THE DIAMONDS
OF GHOST BAYOU

A Tony Boudreaux Mystery

Other Books by Kent Conwell

Angelina Showdown
Atascocita Gold
Bowie's Silver
The Crystal Skull Murders
Death in the Distillery
Death in the French Quarter
Extracurricular Murder
Galveston
Grave for a Dead Gunfighter
Gunfight at Frio Canyon
A Hanging in Hidetown
Junction Flats Drifter
Llano River Valley
Murder Among Friends
Red River Crossing
The Riddle of Mystery Inn
Shootout on the Sabine
Texas Orphan Train
The Puzzle of Piri Reis
An Unmarked Grave
Vicksburg

THE DIAMONDS
OF GHOST BAYOU

•

Kent Conwell

AVALON BOOKS
NEW YORK

Library of Congress Cataloging-in-Publication Data

Conwell, Kent.
    The diamonds of Ghost Bayou : a Tony Boudreaux mystery
/ Kent Conwell.
        p.   cm.
    ISBN 978-0-8034-7618-9 (hardcover : alk. paper)
    1. Diamonds—Fiction.   2. Serial murders—Fiction.
3. Bayous—Fiction.   4. Teche, Bayou (La.)—Fiction.
5. New Orleans (La.)—Fiction.   6. Boudreaux, Tony
(Fictitious character)—Fiction.   I. Title.
    PS3553.O547D53 2011
    813'.54—dc22

                                        2011025772

PRINTED IN THE UNITED STATES OF AMERICA
ON ACID-FREE PAPER
BY RR DONNELLEY, HARRISONBURG, VIRGINIA

To Kenli, my first granddaughter.
May she grow to be a strong and independent
woman like her mom.

And to my wife, Gayle.

Chapter One

Even after a week back in sunny Austin, I was still shivering, not only from the frigid days I had spent in the snow-covered peaks of the Sangre de Cristos Mountains, but from trying to dodge three goons intent on burying me under a hundred feet of snow.

I decided it was time to take some vacation. The last several months, with exotic maps and crystal skulls and saving my old man from a murder rap, had kept me busier than a Sixth Street wino hustling quarters for a bottle of Thunderbird.

My wishes were not to be.

Strange, how what a person wants and what he gets are almost never the same. I've often wondered if this was some sort of cosmic law designed by the gods just to keep us in our place.

My first day back, I toyed with the idea of a skiing trip to Colorado, but my time in New Mexico had cured me of even the slightest proclivity for snow and wet and cold. About that time, my old friend Jack Edney and his wife, Diane, my ex-wife, invited me to visit their new vacation home on Bayou Fantôme, just off the Bayou Teche Scenic Byway in Louisiana.

Naturally, I'd refused, not because she was my ex-wife, but because a few months earlier, when I was trying to locate a missing map down in San Antonio, she'd made a pass at me. Of course, at the time, she was angry with Jack and had had a tad too much to drink. Still, I was kind of antsy around her.

I finally decided simply to play the vacation by ear. I'd get up in the morning, spin a bottle, and just head in that direction. I might even visit a few Civil War battlefields, a journey I had long pondered, and I could start at Vicksburg.

There was nothing keeping me in Austin; my significant other, Janice Coffman-Morrison, was on a cruise with her Aunt Beatrice, owner and CEO of Chalk Hills Distillery; my cat, A.B., never returned after taking off on a courting trip; my old man had hit the rails again; and my boss suggested some time off.

So, I was free and unfettered, and the road was calling. I felt like a schoolboy when that last bell rang dismissing school for the summer.

That's when I got the phone call. It was from Diane. She was crying. She was in Priouxville, Louisiana. Jack had been beaten severely. He was in the hospital. "He needs you, Tony. Please. He needs you. I need you."

Talk about mixed emotions running rampant in both directions. I stammered, "Calm down, Diane. What happened? How bad is he? Can I talk to him?"

"No. He's in a coma," she replied hurriedly, one word tumbling over another. "I don't know what happened except he went outside to check on some noises, and someone beat him up something terrible, terrible."

Drawing a deep breath, I hesitated for all of two seconds. "No problem. Where are you now?"

"At the hospital with Jack." She hesitated and then, her voice beginning to tremble, added, "I don't know the address. It's the Bayou Teche Hospital here in Priouxville."

Trying to calm her, I said, "Look, Jack's tough. He'll be all right. Just pull yourself together, you hear?" I glanced at my watch: ten o'clock. "I ought to be there around four this afternoon. Just get hold of yourself. I'll see you later."

I stared at the receiver after hanging up, wondering if I had made the right decision.

If it had just been Jack, I would have had no second thoughts. Diane was the problem. Still, Jack and I went way back to Madison High School in Austin, where I taught English and he coached football and track.

Literature and sports. An unusual combination, but we'd hit

it off from the first. Over the years, he'd helped me out of some jams, and I had done the same for him. The one time I didn't help him when perhaps I should have was when he told me he was going to marry my ex-wife.

Instead, I kept my mouth shut, reminding myself I was as much to blame as Diane for the divorce.

It was amicable and fair as divorces went. I got my pickup, my clothes, and Oscar, a brain-damaged Albino Barb in a forty-gallon aquarium. She walked away with her car, clothes, all the furniture, and our meager savings account. Diane was one of those unfortunates with the proverbial Champagne taste on a beer budget.

In fact, Jack even asked me if I minded if he proposed to her. That's the kind of friend he is. Not eager to dredge up old aches and pains, I gave him my blessing.

Taking a deep breath, I told myself it was the right decision but maybe not the most prudent.

I dialed the office and cleared the next couple of weeks with my boss, Marty Blevins, owner of Blevins' Security.

Fifteen minutes later, I was on Highway 290 in my Chevrolet Silverado, heading east for Houston and the I-10, on which I would stay to Lafayette, Louisiana. From there, I'd cut south, straight into the heart of Acadiana.

During my drive, a thousand questions bounced around my skull. Jack, by his own admission, was a lover, not a fighter—a wise decision, since he was as broad as he was short. Personally, I fully supported his philosophy, although not by any stretch of the imagination could I consider myself a lover, nor a fighter, even though I'd been in more than my share of brawls.

I always looked for an alternative to physical violence, but sometimes it didn't exist. I'd learned the hard way that "fair fight" was the ultimate oxymoron. I never fought fair. I fought to win.

Now, I knew from experience just how locals along the bayous felt about newcomers invading their domain. They resented outsiders and made their feelings known in various ways. Jack was the kind to overcome those prejudices.

When he'd mentioned the idea of a vacation home on a Louisiana bayou, I told him some of the problems he might face, such as resentment among the locals, an abundance of snakes, squadrons of vicious mosquitoes, floods, the distance from civilization, an almost alien culture, and half a dozen other drawbacks.

Diane wasn't crazy about the idea, but he was not to be swayed. The locals he would win over; he contracted with a pest company to spray repellents for snakes; he put out mosquito zappers; and he came up with answers for the other redundant downsides.

Turning off at Lafayette, I stayed on Highway 90 instead of taking the more scenic route. Actually, most highways south of I-10 could be considered scenic; they are lined with drooping oaks laden with swaying Spanish moss, harkening back to antebellum days of tiny-waisted young debutantes in billowing gowns swirling round and round at gala cotillions.

Diane hurried toward me when I eased open the door to Jack's room. She hugged me and pressed her cheek against mine. "Oh, Tony. I'm so glad you're here." Other than her dress being slightly rumpled and a couple of wisps of her brown hair out of place, the only way you could tell she'd been under a strain was her red-rimmed eyes. She had always been meticulous about her appearance, and since I was the consummate slob, the handwriting was on the wall even before we married; we were just too much in lust to bother to read it.

I peered at the bowling ball covered with a sheet. An IV dripped slowly into a purple-splotched arm. "How is he?" His face was a mass of bruises and swelling. His jaw was wired shut. One forearm was in a cast.

"Stable," she whispered. "The doctor just left."

Wincing as I stared down at my old friend, I asked, "He still in a coma?"

She hesitated. "It isn't a coma. I thought they said that, but I don't think it is. He woke a couple of hours back, then went back to sleep."

I glanced sidelong at her, skeptical of her explanation. After all, I'd been married to her. She was sort of flaky. I looked back at Jack. He seemed to be resting as peacefully as possible. I whispered, "Let's get some coffee. You need a break."

She smiled up at me weakly.

In the small cafeteria, I got us coffee from the vending machine and doctored hers with sweetener and cream. Taking a chair across the table from her, I said, "Tell me what happened."

She sipped her coffee and then set it down. "I don't know a lot. We were in bed. We heard noises out on the porch, which goes all the way around the house. Jack thought it was probably raccoons or possums, so he went out." She began wringing her hands. "I told him to turn on the light, but he said there was no need. I heard some thuds and groans. I figured he was chasing whatever it was around the porch. Then he screamed. I hurried to the living room and switched on the floodlights, but there wasn't anyone out there."

"Then what?"

She continued wringing her hands. "I-I was scared, but I pushed open the storm door and saw Jack lying at the bottom of the stairs."

I grimaced. The flights of stairs leading up to the porches of those bayou houses were at least ten feet or higher. "What about Jack?"

"He was on his back, groaning."

"Did he say anything?"

She stopped wringing her hands and looked up at me. "Yes."

I leaned forward. "What?"

She replied hoarsely, "Diamonds!"

Chapter Two

Diamonds?" The word surprised me.

She ducked her head, the ends of her short brown hair falling down on either side of her face. "That's what he said, 'diamonds.'"

"Anything else?"

Lifting her gaze to my eyes, she replied, "No." She shrugged. "Well, maybe a few curses."

Now that sounded like Jack. "Diamonds, huh? That doesn't make any sense to me. Does it to you?"

"No," she said softly, shaking her head.

"What about the police? You notify them?"

Woodenly she replied, "Yes. The sheriff asked the same kind of questions." She drew a deep breath and leaned back in her chair. "Maybe more. I forget. It feels like we've been in the hospital for days."

A wave of sympathy washed over me. I patted her hand. "Look. Let me take you out to the house. You can get a good night's rest. I'll stay with Jack."

She squeezed my hand and with a wan smile, replied, "No. I want to stay with him. You stay at the house tonight."

I studied her. For a fleeting instant, I wondered if she would have felt the same devotion toward me when we were married. I pushed the slings and arrows of envy aside. She and Jack were made for each other. What do they call it, soul mates? She and I were opposites. She was a town girl, and I was a country boy. And even in a small town like Church Point, there is a cultural difference. While some say opposites attract, my experience has been that whatever the magnetic attraction is between opposites, it quickly wears off or shorts out. I learned it the hard way.

"If that's what you want."

"It is."

"All right. Just write down the directions. I'll stop in to see the sheriff first and then check things out at your place. I'll give you a call later and drop back by. We'll go grab a bite to eat. Okay?"

She fumbled in her purse. "Here are the house keys."

Priouxville straddled Highway 87. There were five intersections in town, all with signal lights, none of which were coordinated with the others, so it was next to impossible to make it through the small community without stopping at least three times. In the middle of the third block sat the courthouse, a gray stone edifice that reminded me of our Catholic church back in Church Point. Across the street was the sheriff's office.

Perhaps a dozen vehicles, mostly pickups, were parked along the curbs of the five-block-long village. I pulled up beside a police cruiser outside the sheriff's office.

A few hundred yards beyond the small village flowed a broad bayou. I didn't know if it was part of Bayou Teche or one of the other numerous bayous throughout this neck of the woods.

All I wanted to do was meet the sheriff and see if he had any leads on those goons who had jumped Jack.

A tall man in a brown uniform looked up from behind a desk when I opened the door. I glanced at the nameplate on his desk. "Sheriff Lacoutrue?"

He looked up at me with intense black eyes; then a broad grin split his dark face. "At your service, *mon ami*. Sheriff Thertule Lacoutrue."

I introduced myself and offered my hand. He gestured to a chair. "*S'il vous plaît*, have a seat." He plopped back down in his swivel chair. "What can I do for you, Mr. Boudreaux?"

"A friend of mine, Jack Edney, was assaulted last night."

He peered up at me from under his eyebrows suspiciously. "*Oui*. What does that have to do with you?"

"His wife, Diane, asked me to come. We were good friends back in Austin. Jack and I taught school together." He nodded, and I continued. "I was wondering if you had any idea who assaulted him."

For several moments, the dark-complexioned man looked me over. "You still be a teacher, Mr. Boudreaux?"

"No. I work for Blevins' Security in Austin."

"A PI, huh?"

"Yeah." I hastened to add, "And I know enough not to try to butt into your business, Sheriff. With Jack laid up in the hospital, his wife is by herself." He lifted a sly eyebrow, an insinuation that bristled the hair on the back of my neck. "She's a city girl. Out there on the bayou by herself, she'd go to pieces. You know what I mean?"

His smile faded slightly. "*Oui*."

"If you're wondering about me, check with Jimmy LeBlanc. Last year, I tracked a missing man over to Bagotville. I contacted Officer Jimmy LeBlanc at the parish office and asked his permission to continue the case."

An amused gleam filled his eyes. "Me, I think you want to look for the *agresseur*."

I frowned. I grew up in a Cajun French community, but the word *agresseur* was a new one on me.

"Mugger," Sheriff Lacoutrue explained.

"Oh." I paused, then added, "I just want to ask a few questions, like any citizen, that's all."

A scowl darkened his face. "*Oui,* I check with Jimmy, but even so, me, I think maybe this is something you should leave to us."

I said nothing, letting the expression on my face ask the question that was on my mind.

The sheriff continued, "Me, I check the house this morning. I see nothing broken, only the head knocked from the Virgin Mother. The doors, they locked, and blinds drawn."

"Vandals, you think?"

He hesitated. He tapped his chest. "*Mais non*. I don't believe it be vandals. All they want is to tear up and run away, not stop and beat this friend of yours." He paused and then added, "It might be the *agresseur.*"

"Mugger?"

"*Oui.* Over the last few months, we have three murders in our parish, all by beatings. Last one, he be ex-con." He shook his head and clucked his tongue. "Thibodeaux, he be my deputy, he think it the *agresseur,* the mugger, who be responsible for your friend's trouble. He think maybe it be more than one *agresseur.* I don't agree at first, but now . . ." He shrugged. "As much as I don't like to say it, I think Thibodeaux, he be right, even if these *agresseurs,* they don't have the same m.o."

I leaned forward. "How's that?"

"All the others, they by themselves in secluded areas. They never come close to houses." He paused and shrugged. "So why this time? Who can say? Maybe they become braver."

"Then why didn't they finish the job?"

"Maybe because your friend's wife, she turn on the lights."

"I understand. So, do you have any objection if I ask a few questions? Anything I run across is yours first."

"No. Me, I have no problem at all with what you say you want to do." He paused, and his face grew hard. "If LeBlanc say the word."

I had planned on bringing up Jack's mention of diamonds, but I figured I'd better get out of there before the sheriff had a change of mind.

It was almost six thirty when I left the sheriff's office. I guessed there was about forty-five minutes left of daylight, which should be plenty of time to reach their home on Bayou Fantôme. Back in Austin, when Jack told me the location of the house, I'd kept my mouth shut. While I am far from glib in the Cajun French patois, I knew the English translation for Bayou Fantôme was "Ghost Bayou." And in that neck of the Louisiana woods, there was a reason for most names given by the old-timers.

The narrow macadam road led into a dark forest thickly populated with pine and occasional oak, obviously one of the thousands of tree farms throughout Louisiana. The tall pines formed a canopy fifty feet overhead, giving the impression of driving through a tunnel.

As dusk drew near, a few rabbits ventured onto the shoulder. Back off the road, a deer looked up as I passed. I glanced down the road. I was close. Just around the next curve, according to Diane's directions.

A deer leaped out in front of me. I slammed on the Silverado's brakes. The tires screeched and then hit a stretch of sand washed over the road from the last heavy rain. I slid into a ditch on the left side of the road.

I slammed the truck into reverse, but the wheels just spun. Cursing under my breath, I hopped out and stared at the front wheel buried hub-deep in the soft mud. I kicked the wheel and cursed some more, dreading the walk back to town.

Abruptly, the wheezing and rattling of an old truck broke the silence. I looked around. A hundred feet down the narrow road, an ancient pickup almost identical to my Grand-père Moise's 1949 Chevrolet came out of a dirt road and turned in my direction.

The pickup ground to a halt beside me. The bed was full of scrap metal and aluminum cans. A cigarette dangling between his lips, a wrinkled old man peered out the window and cackled. "Need some help?"

Talk about a rhetorical question. I played the game. "You bet."

Leaving the sixty-year-old pickup idling and gasping, he clambered out and shuffled around to me. He was skinnier than a fence post, and his overalls and denim shirt hung on him like a scarecrow's. He paused, looked up at me, and then glanced at the wheel mired in the ditch.

Without a word, he turned back to his pickup and fished in one corner of the bed and pulled out a chain. "Put one end on your tow ball," he said, glancing at the trailer hitch on my back bumper. He deftly formed a large loop in the other end of the chain and draped it around the tow ball on his truck.

Two minutes later, I was out.

I wanted to pay him, but he refused. I knew he would. Those old-timers always do.

He eyed me warily. "You be a stranger?"

"Yeah. Name's Tony Boudreaux from up around Church Point."

The wrinkled old man took a deep drag off his unfiltered cigarette. "They call me Rouly. I got me a place back down that road—right on the bayou." He blew out a stream of smoke. "You looking for somebody?"

I hooked my thumb over my shoulder. "Visiting some friends down the road."

His face clouded with suspicion. "Ain't nobody live there. The place, it be filled with haints. Has been since old man Prioux sell it." He paused, concentrating. "Let's see, that was—" His face lit. "*Oui.* Nineteen fifty. I remember because that one, he sell it the year after I buy this truck of mine."

I was about to dismiss the old man as a loony, one of those who had lived in the woods too long with only alligators and snakes to keep him company.

He continued, tapping his chest with his middle finger. "Me, Augustus J. Rouly, I see the *feu follet;* it play there with the loup-garou. Me, I see lights at night."

I ignored his fancies. "My friends bought the house. Those are probably the lights you see."

And he ignored my explanation. "It good I find you. Just a couple nights ago, old L. Q. Benoit was walking down this very road. The loup-garou, he jump him. He turn himself into a horse and kill Benoit dead by stomping on him."

Loup-garou, like the *feu follet,* was nothing more than an old-time Cajun superstition. The loup-garou, or werewolf, of Cajun myth can be any kind of bird or beast. Some are even good spirits, but most, for whatever reason, are dark and treacherous. I guessed Rouly's loup-garou was probably the mugger or muggers of which Sheriff Lacoutrue had spoken.

Old Rouly cackled. "That Benoit, he didn't have no time to get himself even one big drunk." When he saw the frown on my face, he explained. "Benoit, he come back from prison. He just come from the sheriff and the deputy, and he come to my shack, and me and him, we have a drink to celebrate his parole, and then he go off to his shack. They find him next morning."

Like all the old-timers, Rouly could probably talk around the clock, but I had business at hand. I glanced at the sky, noting the fading signs of dusk. I shook his hand. "Thanks again, Mr. Rouly. Maybe I'll see you around."

I was still laughing at the odd old man when I rounded the bend and spotted Diane and Jack's house. But what really got my attention were the two men running down the stairs and racing toward two boats moored at the dock. One of the goons was bald.

I floored the pickup. The engine screamed. The truck leaped forward. Another hundred feet and the macadam ended, but a dirt road continued along the bayou. I shot onto the road and angled toward the dock. I slammed on the brakes just as the two roared away in a yellow Stratos, leaving a wide, foamy wake behind them.

I recognized the second boat as Jack's, a Mako 191 I helped him pick out at Carrier's Marine in Austin a couple of months earlier. I raced down the pier, threw off the stern and bow lines, and then jumped in behind the center console. I cursed. No keys.

I stuck the throttle into neutral and then dropped to my knees and peered under the console. One of the questionable skills I'd developed on my job as a PI was hot-wiring vehicles, and the Mako was a snap. Fifteen seconds later, the ninety-horsepower Mercury roared to life.

I jammed the throttle onto full power. The stern dipped, and the nineteen-foot Mako leaped forward.

Three feet later, the speeding boat slammed to an abrupt halt, throwing me halfway over the windshield.

Chapter Three

I t took me a moment to gather my senses and climb off the windshield that I was painfully straddling. By then, the sound of the retreating outboard was fading into the dark swamps. I looked around to see what had jerked the boat into such an abrupt halt. I was stunned to see the big engine tilted forward, its lower unit parallel to the water, with a massive chain linked around it, and the other end fastened to one of the piers supporting the dock.

I shook my head and muttered in wonder, "Jack, what in the blazes was on your mind?"

Cursing softly, I reached for the chain. I glanced over my shoulder and spotted a man about fifty yards deep into the bayou. He was standing in a boat, sort of like a canoe, watching. I blinked, and he vanished. For several moments, I stood staring into the growing shadows where I had seen him. Or had I? This time of evening, swamp shadows played eerie tricks.

I turned back to the business at hand. After using the chain to pull the boat back to the dock in the quickly fading light, I checked the Mako's transom, surprised that the impact hadn't ripped it off.

A soft rumble of thunder rolled through the swamps. I glanced back to the south and caught a jagged trunk of lightning slashing down from a thunderhead outlined with silver. From a compartment under the casting deck, I pulled out the boat cover and quickly snapped it on.

Pulling my truck back under the four-car carport south of the house, I locked it and looked up at the house. The lower concourse was covered with white lattice through which myriad roses wound and twisted their branches. That was cute.

13

The single-story house on ten-foot piers was gray with sparkling white trim. Thick cypress shingles covered the hipped roof that extended beyond the walls to cover the porch on all four sides of the house and the French doors that opened onto the porch from each room. All very cute.

The porch railings and balusters, as the stairs, were constructed of cypress. Though they were painted white to match the other trim, the stair details were rough and awkward, a jarring presence against the smooth details of the porch railings.

They were not cute.

Later I would learn they were part of the original house, but regardless of their history, they were as out of place as a lump of coal in a handful of diamonds.

I slipped my .38 from the locked toolbox in the rear of the pickup and dropped it into my pocket.

Statues of the Virgin Mother stood at either side of the stairs. The one on the left had no head; it lay on the ground beside it. I picked it up to check its fit, figuring on using some concrete cement to fasten it back. I was surprised to see that the head was hollow, and then I realized the entire statue was made of some sort of fiberglass. Superglue would do the job.

I chuckled. *Superglue and duct tape, the adhesive's that held modern man together.*

Warily, I climbed the stairs. I could feel my heart thudding against my chest, and my dry lips told me the rest of my respiratory system was speeding up from the tension.

I opened the storm door and then unlocked the main door. With the blinds drawn, it was dark inside. I felt along the wall for the light switch.

My blood pressure dropped instantly when the light came on. I gazed around a neat living area, as modern and up-to-date as the newest home in any gated community.

I had expected the place to be a wreck, but none of the rooms appeared disturbed, which meant that either the two goons I'd seen leaving were very careful or that my arrival had stopped their search before it had begun.

A fireplace separated the spacious living area from the dining room. Off the dining area was the kitchen. And from the living room, a hallway led to four bedrooms, each with its own bath, including both shower and tub.

Satisfied that I was all by myself and that no bogeyman would jump out of a closet, I made sure all the doors and windows were locked.

With a grimace, I remembered I had promised Diane we'd go out for dinner. I hated to leave. For all I knew, someone was out there right now watching. If I drove away, they'd fall onto the house like vultures. I drew a deep breath. In my business, lies and half-truths are accepted practices. So I decided I'd tell her I had car trouble. I didn't figure she needed any more worry than she had.

I called her and said all was well. "How's Jack?"

"Oh, Tony. I'm so excited. He woke up after you left. I managed to get some soup down him. It's hard with that broken jaw. He had to use a straw. One arm is in a cast, and the other is full of IVs. I had to feed him."

I suppressed a laugh. Jack was a meat-and-potatoes man. "Is he awake now?"

"No. But I told him you were here." She hesitated and then continued. "If you don't mind, Tony, I don't feel much like eating. I've got a Coke and a bag of chips. I'd sooner stay here with Jack in case he wakes up again. I'll come out tomorrow and get a change of clothes."

"Fine. Look, things are going okay. Nothing to worry about. You get a good night's rest. I'll be in first thing in the morning." I paused. "When you reported the assault to the sheriff, did you mention anything about the diamonds?"

Diane paused. "I'm not sure. I don't think so. Why? Should I?"

"I don't know. For the time being, let's just keep it between us, okay?"

I replaced the receiver and looked around the neat living room. My stomach growled, and I realized I hadn't eaten since the hamburger in Vinton just inside the Louisiana border.

Louisiana is a gambling state, and I hadn't been able to resist dropping a few bucks into the slots while I munched my burger. Usually, I have fair luck on the slots, but today I'd bombed out. I hoped that wasn't a portent of things to come.

To still my growling stomach, I had a peanut butter sandwich and a glass of milk.

I awoke when the storm hit, around midnight, a typical spring thunderstorm with towering black thunderheads continually lanced by brilliant orange and whites slashes of lightning.

I went to the window and watched as the magnificent storm passed, its great gusts raking through the spidery cypress, bending the limbs and making the leaves dance. Crashing bursts of light revealed the dark swamp in an eerie but striking relief.

Down at the dock, the Mako, pushed by the wind and waves, rocked against its rubber bumpers. During the frequent flashes of lightning, I could see the rain coursing off the boat cover and sluicing into the black waters of Ghost Bayou.

I froze, peering into the stormy night. I could have sworn I saw tiny lights deep in the swamp. I blinked once or twice and then squinted again, but the lights had disappeared—if they were ever there.

If you've never awakened to a Louisiana morning after a night storm, you've missed one of life's most beautiful experiences.

I climbed out of bed and threw open the window, drawing in a breath of sweet, clean air. The coffeepot was ready to go, so I flicked it on and headed for the bathroom. Ten minutes later, I poured a cup and took it out onto the porch.

The rain had bathed the lawn and trees and shrubs with a deep green that reminded me of one of Robert Frost's poems. I can't remember the name of the poem now, but I'll never forget the line, "Nature's first green is gold." And as I gazed upon the freshly washed leaves on the massive dark cypress trunks made almost black by the rain, I felt a close kinship with the old poet.

Even the birds were happy. White egrets abounded, some perching on cypress knees only inches from the bulwarks and backfill that Jack had thrown up along the edge of the black water. Blue jays darted through the treetops in swooping dives and curving arcs. And along the shoreline, long-tailed male grackles did their mating dance around their chosen mates.

I drew another deep breath, savoring the sweet thickness of honeysuckle on the morning air, fresh and clean as a newly bathed baby.

And then, from the darkness deep in the swamp, came the alligators, gliding silently beneath the tannic-stained water, their bulbous eyes focused on the egrets and grackles along the shoreline.

Sipping my coffee, I watched as a six-foot alligator glided up to the bulwark and then gracefully eased over the top, eyeing a shiny black grackle dancing around a mousy brown grackle not eight feet from the shore. The birds appeared to ignore the reptile. The alligator, mouth agape, shot forward. The birds scattered. The frustrated reptile jerked its head back and forth once or twice and then lay down, the scales along its spine vibrating.

I downed the remainder of my coffee and went back inside.

Before I left for the hospital, I made certain everything was locked down, not that it would do that much good if someone truly wanted in.

Covered with bruises, Jack was awake. Although still partially sedated, he tried to grin when I walked in, but it was more of a leer. He held up his right hand. I grabbed it and squeezed. "You're getting too old for this kind of nonsense, Jack."

He gave a weak laugh. "Tell me about it."

Diane spoke up. "They came in to give him another shot for the pain, but he begged off. He wanted to talk to you first."

"Well, I'm here, old buddy. What's on your mind?"

He glanced at the door. In a muted, hesitant voice, he asked, "Is the nurse gone?"

"Yeah."

"Good."

"So?"

"Something's going on, Tony. And someone thinks I'm part of it."

I frowned at Diane. "Part of what?"

He blew through his lips in frustration. "That's what I don't know. All I know is that diamonds are involved."

"Diane mentioned them."

His words were slurred. "The other night when those two were beating on me, they kept asking, 'Where's the diamonds? Where's the diamonds?' "

I interrupted him. "There was more than one, then?"

"Yeah. Two of them." He tightened the grip on my hand. "I'm scared for Diane. Don't leave her alone, please. I've seen lights out in the swamp at night, and we've had prowlers around before this happened."

"Prowlers?"

"I had to chain the boat to a pier. I didn't know if they were going to steal it or not, but one early morning, I saw two guys looking at it. They were in another boat."

"What color?"

"Yellow." He tightened his grip on my hand. "Just look after Diane for me, you hear?"

San Antonio flashed into my mind, but I quickly pushed it aside. "Don't worry, pal. She'll be fine." I glanced around at her. Her eyes brimmed with tears.

The door opened, and a slender young woman in flowered scrubs, her blond hair pulled back in a ponytail, entered briskly. "Time for your meds, Mr. Edney. No more putting it off." She smiled at us. "Good morning."

We stepped back as she checked Jack's vital signs, then injected drugs into the IV. "Did you sleep well?"

He forced a wry smile. "With all this stuff in me?"

Within moments of her administering the drugs, Jack slipped into a peaceful sleep. The nurse smiled at us. "He'll sleep for some time now, if you have errands to run."

"I'll follow you," I said outside, as Diane climbed into their Cadillac.

She looked around. "I have to make a stop at the vet's first."
I nodded, puzzled.

When she came out of the vet's, she was cradling a tiny dog with long white hair in her arms. She was cooing to the dog as it was doing its best to lick her face. I don't know what they're called, but the little guy could fit in a woman's purse.

She turned the dog loose in the backseat, but it promptly jumped up front as she slid behind the wheel.

I couldn't help wondering where it had come from; they didn't have a dog when they left Austin to take possession of their new vacation home.

Diane pulled into the carport. As soon as she opened her door, the dog leaped to the ground and, like a white streak, shot across the yard toward the mating grackles, yapping at the top of his lungs.

Diane watched for a moment and then turned to me. "That's Mr. Jay. We bought him last week. He's a miniature cairn terrier."

I watched the energetic little terrier bouncing all over the lawn, scattering one bunch of birds, then dashing after another. "Cute," I said with a shake of my head. "But you know, you've got alligators out there. Your Mr. Jay wouldn't even be a mouthful."

Chapter Four

She waved off my warning. "They wouldn't bother him. Besides, he's too fast for them."

I glanced back at the yapping terrier, reluctant to leave him outside.

Diane continued, "Now, let's go in. I can't wait to take a shower." She seized her blouse between her index finger and thumb and pulled it away from her skin. She shook it. "I feel all greasy and dirty."

Diane and I had been married for a couple of years, so I was more than familiar with her penchant for cleanliness, which at times I had considered bordering on the obsessive. "All right. I'll open the windows and let in some fresh air."

We mounted the steps, and I unlocked the door. Back in the yard, Mr. Jay was yap-yap-yapping. I pushed the door open for Diane, and she headed directly for the master bathroom. I called after her. "After I throw open the windows, I'll check on the boat."

With San Antonio winking at me, the last thing I wanted was to be in the house while she was showering.

As usual in Louisiana, by midmorning the sun had burned away the clean freshness of dawn, and steam was beginning to rise from the soaked gumbo soil.

I watched the yapping pup as I made my way to the Mako, several times scanning the dark swamp water for alligators. Mr. Jay was in dog heaven: all the birds he could chase, and all the room to chase them in.

When I stepped onto the dock, I glanced into the swamp

where I thought I had seen a man the day before. The only movement was the Spanish moss waving idly in the faint breeze.

Unzipping the boat cover, I climbed over the gunwale, plopped down behind the wheel, and stared at the gauges. For twenty minutes, I sat in the captain's seat, staring, unseeing, at the gauges, going back over the events of the last couple of days. The only obvious conclusion I could draw at the time was that there must be diamonds somewhere on the premises and somebody wanted them.

I had two leads: the two jokers running from the house, and the yellow Stratos, the same color boat that Jack had spotted. I guessed it had to be moored along the river somewhere, and I decided to see if I could run it down. Just then, Diane stepped out onto the porch and waved. She wore a white blouse and matching shorts. I waved back. "I'll fix some lunch," she shouted. "Ten minutes."

Though the early-morning nip was gone, the air flowing through the open windows kept us cool as we sat in the living area munching on tuna fish sandwiches, chips, and soft drinks. The TV was on the local news. Outside, Mr. Jay continued barking.

I reached for my Dr Pepper. "What time do you want to go back to the hospital?"

She was sitting on the couch with her tanned legs folded under her. "Maybe later this afternoon. Jack needs rest, not visitors, don't you think?" She looked at me innocently.

Outside, Mr. Jay was still yapping.

"Oh, yeah, yeah." My mind raced. I had no intention of spending the afternoon with Diane in this large, empty house. Yet, I had promised Jack I'd look after her. "Tell you what," I said. "Why don't we take a leisurely trip up the river today? Give you a chance to see your neighbors. We can take our cells in case the hospital calls."

She clapped her hands like a schoolgirl. "That sounds wonderful. Should I make us something to eat?"

"No," I hastily replied. "We won't be gone that long. We'll just see what's up there and then get back early so we can spend time with Jack this evening."

Mr. Jay's yap turned into a startled yelp.

By the time we reached the front door, he was sitting on top of the stairs looking back at the bayou where a five-foot alligator stood motionless on the shore, staring up at the trembling pup.

"Oh, dear," Diane exclaimed, hurrying to the shaking dog. "Look at his little tail. That horrid creature bit him."

I suppressed a grin. The pup was lucky. All Mr. Alligator had done was chomp down on the tail, but it was so tiny—a stub, really—and the pup had managed to jerk it loose, peeling away some skin. He was lucky it hadn't ended up a lot stubbier.

I opened the door as she brought the pup inside and headed for the bathroom. "He'll be okay," I said above his whining and her cooing voice. But, I told myself, he'll never venture down those stairs again.

Swamps and forests are misleading. From a distance, their cool shadows promise an inviting respite from the hot sun. In reality, they are usually hot and oppressive because the thick canopy of cypress and water oak holds in the heat and humidity. The air is suffocating.

Only the uncharted waterways crisscrossing the swamp offered a modicum of relief, and then only because of the forward movement of the watercraft.

When I helped Diane into the boat, I heard Mr. Jay barking from inside the house. "I opened the door for him to come out, but he didn't want to."

"Can't blame the little fellow," I said.

"I think I'll take him back to the vet's until Jack comes home. What do you think?"

"Yeah. That's a good idea."

I raised the special-ordered canopy on the Mako, and we enjoyed a gentle breeze generated by our ten-mile-an-hour speed. On the left, the shoreline, thick with oak and pine and an occasional cypress, sloped gently upward to a six- or seven-foot crest above the waterline. About halfway up was a line of debris marking the last high water in the swamp. From time to time, dark and narrow bayous cut through the shore and wound deeper into the forest.

On our right spread the deep and uncharted Marais de Fantôme, Ghost Swamp, which flowed into the Atchafalaya Swamp. The swamp abounded in myth and legends spread by the old-timers since the time of the dispersal of the Acadians from Nova Scotia in 1755, when one solitary band of the exiles wandered into and explored the wilds of Louisiana.

As we glided silently along the river, the bellowing of alligators and harrumphing of bullfrogs echoed from the dark shadows of Ghost Swamp.

"Oh, look!" Diane exclaimed, pointing to an eight-foot alligator sunning on the bank. As we drew close, the reptile slid silently into the water. The sight of dazzling white egrets perched on cypress knees thrilled her as much as the sinuous wake of a water moccasin repelled her.

Despite the canopy of leaves and the gentle breeze, we began to swelter. Perspiration beaded on our foreheads. She dabbed at hers and gestured to the shade along the edge of the swamp cast by the tree crowns extending over the river. "Wouldn't it be cooler over there?" She indicated the inviting shadows dappling the brown-tinted water.

I pointed to the protruding limbs overhead. "You bet, but what if one of those falls?"

She gasped when she spotted several coiled snakes sunning on limbs high above the water.

A few minutes later, she shifted in her seat. Her bare legs made popping noises as they pulled away from the plastic to which her perspiration had stuck them. "It doesn't look like we have any neighbors."

I was thinking the same thing, but the yellow Stratos had to have come from somewhere, and I had yet to run across a boat ramp or any spot that gave evidence of a launch site. The few bayous we had noticed cutting off the river appeared too narrow and shallow. No, I told myself. Whatever we were looking for was still ahead. "Let's give it a few more minutes."

Around the next bend, we spotted a neat house with a porch on all four sides. It stood on twelve-foot piers. A flight of steps led down to a dock at which were moored a single powerboat and a pirogue. An older man and woman squatted on the pier, a basket between them. As soon as we rounded the bend, they looked up.

I headed directly for them.

Diane gasped. "You're not going over there, are you? Those . . . those are swamp people."

I laughed. "Don't worry, they're not going to make you dance with snakes or anything like that." I waved and eased back on the throttle. As I drew near, I saw they had been peeling and deveining shrimp. "Hello!" I shouted, shifting into neutral, and then reverse, to keep from bumping the pier.

Their eyes wary, they remained silent. I gestured to Diane. "This is Diane Edney. She and her husband bought the gray house downriver from you. I'm Tony Boudreaux."

The woman remained in her squat when the man stood. A wiry little man with a thick head of straight black hair, blacker than the inside of an alligator's belly, tapped his fingers to his chest. "Me, I be Clerville Naquin. This here be my wife, Zozette."

I looked at the shrimp in the basket and the swirls of catfish and alligator beneath the pier feeding on the discarded shrimp heads. "Nice-looking shrimp, Mr. Naquin. What are they, about twenty count or so?"

"*Oui.*"

His wife, Zozette, just stared at us. I glanced at Diane, who was chewing her bottom lip and eyeing Zozette.

It didn't appear they harbored much of a desire for idle chit-chat. Before I could ask about the yellow powerboat, a battered Ranger outboard rounded a bend to the north and headed toward us. In its prime the twenty-foot boat had probably been white, but now, covered with years of mud, rotted vegetation, as well as fish and shrimp slime, it looked almost gray.

"That be August and Dolzin, my boys. They been shrimping and crabbing. Dolzin, he works at T-Ball Stables on the side."

By now, I'd eased our boat up against the pier. Diane tugged on my arm. Under her breath, she whispered, "Tony, let's go." I heard her shiver.

"In a minute," I muttered through the side of my lips.

The shrimp boat nudged the pier. One of the young men leaped off, tied up the boat, and then stared at us warily. He wore no shirt, and his muscles rippled under his dark skin.

Clerville introduced us. The two young men nodded briefly.

I cleared my throat. "I know you have work to do, Mr. Naquin, so I won't bother you any longer. Just one question if you don't mind. Do you folks know anyone with a yellow Stratos, a newer model?"

He frowned as he concentrated. The two boys folded their arms over their chests and glared at me defiantly. Finally, Clerville spoke. "Me, I see many like that on the bayou." His sons uttered their agreement.

From the porch above, a guttural voice called out, "You be them city folk what bought the old Prioux place?"

I looked up and spotted a man in shorts leaning against the rail, a beer in one hand. The sun had baked his skin almost as dark as his hair, which was straight, not curly like that of the pure Cajun. I glanced at Diane, but she was as puzzled as I. "It's the gray house downriver, if that's what you mean."

As he looked straight at me, a satisfied smirk played over his lips. "Me, I know you."

"Tony?" Diane said, looking at me in surprise.

I shrugged. "I've got no idea what he's talking about."

Chapter Five

T hat be Valsin, my oldest," explained Clerville.

I called out, "You must be mistaken. We've never met."

He bounced down the steps to the pier. He wore a bloody skinning knife on his hip. "I see you when you almost sink the boat."

Then I remembered. The figure out in the swamps, the one I wasn't certain I had seen. "Yeah, yeah. Now I remember. You were out in the swamp."

While there was absolutely no physical difference in the musculature between him and his brothers, the crow's-feet fanning out from his eyes and the furrows in his leathery cheeks were mute evidence that he was the oldest. "And you, *mon ami,* almost lose a motor." He glanced past me and spoke in a dialect with which I was not familiar. There were Cajun phrases in it, but the other words, phrases, and various nuances were, as the Roman soldier might have said, Greek to me. His family laughed, and I knew they were laughing at me.

Putting my hands out to my sides, I shrugged and sheepishly replied, "*Ane muet.*" *Dumb donkey.*

Valsin leaned off the pier and offered me his beer. I declined. While not always successful, I did try to observe my AA vows.

Of course, my job didn't help. Much of my work was on the seamy underside of our society. There, hard beverages flow like the Mississippi River. So I faced a daily battle.

But it was growing easier. At least it seemed that way.

Valsin insisted I take his beer, but I shook my head. Changing the subject, I said, "If you saw me almost tear the transom out of the Mako, then you had to see the Stratos."

"*Oui*. I see it."

"Do you know where it is?"

He glanced at his father. The smug smile faded. "They not good people."

"Then you do know where I can find it!"

He hesitated and again glanced at his father.

Clerville looked upriver.

"I show you," Valsin announced, leaping lightly from the pier onto the deck of our boat.

Diane froze, her eyes fixed on the bloody knife on his hip.

He pointed upriver. "There."

I eased into the river and shoved the throttle forward. The Mako's bow rose, and moments later we slid onto a smooth plane. The powerful boat sliced through the water. I glanced at Diane. The expression on her face vacillated between fear and panic. I winked at her. "Everything's all right. Don't worry."

I don't know if I said that to make her feel better or to reassure myself. The bloodstained leather sheath holding his knife remained in the periphery of my vision.

Valsin stood behind us, legs spread. He held on to the back of the bench seat with one hand. Ahead, the river forked. "Take the left, you."

The fork narrowed and swung into a wide bend. I spotted the Golden Crystal Casino as we went around the bend, a sprawling, six-story glass and brick showplace, on the west end of which was a mile-and-a-half racetrack with grandstands.

"In there," he said, pointing to a second fork that curved back to the right into the casino's marina. Around two dozen boats were moored, most in the forty- to fifty-foot Grady White or Trophy class, far removed from the nineteen-footer we were bouncing about in.

I glanced over the boats, failing to spot the yellow Stratos. "I don't see it."

Valsin gestured to a tan metal building at the end of one ramp of the mooring docks. "There. In the boat shed."

We motored slowly up the short waterway and eased to a halt in front of the shed. Just as he said, a yellow Stratos sat rocking on the water in one of the stalls. I looked up at him. "How do you know for sure?"

He touched his middle finger to his chest. "Me, I know. I see that boat many times. This be the one." He pointed to a ten-inch-long scar in the transom. "That how I know."

Diane's face was taut with fear. I leaned over and patted her hand gripping the console. "Everything's all right. We're going back now. Okay?"

She forced a weak smile.

After backing up, I headed for the bayou.

During the run back to the Naquins', I asked Valsin about his trips into the swamps.

He trapped and hunted while his brothers crabbed and fished. Above the purr of the powerful Mercury outboard, he added, "I see much from back in the swamp. Those in the boat, that not be the first time they go to the house." He shrugged. "Three times in the last two months, I see them two."

Diane glanced at me, alarm evident in her eyes.

We pulled up to the pier at his place, and he invited us in for a shrimp boil. "*Mes amis,* the shrimp—it is delicious. And the potatoes. They be soft and hot, and the corn—" He rolled his eyes and shook his. "*Délicieux.*"

Had I been alone, I would have taken him up on the offer, but we needed to get back to the hospital. "Thanks," I said. "Maybe another time. Her husband is in the hospital," I added, not wanting them to feel slighted.

I had already made my plans for the evening. As soon as I got Diane back to the hospital, I planned on paying the Golden Crystal Casino a visit.

After we pulled away from the Naquin pier, Diane looked around at me sharply and said, "Don't ever do that to me again, you hear?"

Her words surprised me. "Do what?" I was truly puzzled.

"I was so scared of those people, I thought I would faint."

I held my temper. "Come on, Diane. I grew up with those kinds of folks. They're good, decent people."

She shivered. "I don't care. You can't tell what people like that are going to do. Why, I thought that last one was going to cut our throats and dump us in the swamp. No one would have ever found us."

I started to snap back, but I reminded myself that even in high school she had always felt she was better than everyone else. Coolly, I replied, "I'm sorry. Next time I go out, I'll drop you off at the hospital first, okay?" I added the last remark with a hint of bitterness.

"Fine with me," she snapped, mollified.

I fumed for a few minutes, and then in a level voice I said, "Tell me something. Why did you let Jack buy this place if you feel that way?"

"I've always felt that way. You know that."

"I figured you might have changed in the last few years."

"Not that way."

"So? Why did you let Jack buy this place?"

"Because," she replied, "he said if I went along with him, we could take the Winter Tour in Europe this year. Christmas in Munich, the canals in Venice." She drew a deep breath. "So I agreed. After all, it's just a vacation house. He promised we wouldn't spend more than a couple of weeks here whenever we came over." She hesitated. "Besides, Jack will get tired of it like he does all his other toys. I give him a year or so."

In some ways she was a snob, just like in some ways I was a slob. Even as a child she had always dreamed of a better life. I couldn't blame her. What is it they say? *Nothing ventured, nothing gained.*

In the last year or so since she and Jack married, I had often chastised myself for thinking that the only reason she'd married Jack was because he had come into eight million dollars. Maybe I shouldn't have been so hard on myself. Still, they did get along remarkably well. And Jack was happy. Who was I to judge?

Perhaps beneath that balding bowling ball of a man who once did comic gigs on Sixth Street in Austin, she saw the brooding charm and sophistication of a New Age Cary Grant. Maybe that's what she saw, not the eight million.

You bet, I told myself ruefully.

Jack was awake and alert. His bruises were starting to turn a sickly purple and yellow. His clenched teeth garbled his words, frustrating him.

I stood back as Diane leaned over him and touched her lips to his forehead. She caressed his pudgy cheek with her hand. "How are you feeling, sweetheart?"

"Ready to get out of here, that's how," he replied.

I grinned at him. "You ain't the prettiest thing I've seen lately, old buddy."

He winked at me. "Maybe not, but I'll get better. You'll always look like a donkey's rear end."

We all laughed, and the truth is, I was surprised at just how much more energy he showed. "Doc been in?"

"Just left. Says I'm fine. CT scan showed nothing wrong in my head."

Teasing, I replied, "Missing brain didn't bother him, huh?"

He muttered an amicable curse. "Says if I keep doing like I am, I can go home in another couple of days. They'll arrange for a home-health nurse to drop in on me."

"Sounds good to me."

He eased his right arm over his rotund belly, opening his hand. "Thanks for coming over, Tony. You don't know how much I appreciate it."

I squeezed his hand. "No problem." I glanced at Diane. "After I take your wife to supper, I'll drop her off back here. I have a couple errands to run."

"I'm not hungry," she said quickly. "Besides, there's the cafeteria." She smiled coolly. "I'll be fine."

"Whatever you say." Reluctantly, I asked, "You going to spend the night at the house or up here?"

She smiled at Jack. "Here." She indicated the La-Z-Boy recliner in the corner. "I'll be fine right there."

A sense of guilt washed over me. Maybe I was too full of myself. After all, that night back in San Antonio when she made a pass at me, she'd had too many bourbon neats or martinis or whatever she was drinking. "You two need anything, call. You have my cell number."

After leaving the hospital, I pulled into a convenience store, Doquet's Stop N Shop, and filled the Silverado tank. Just as I was finishing, a rusty 1949 Chevrolet pickup rattled in. Augustus J. Rouly. He gave me a gap-toothed grin through the windshield as he parked. He clambered out and slammed the door. "Howdy, boy. See you stayed away from the loup-garou!"

"Stayed inside and locked the door," I replied lightly.

He slipped the nozzle into the gas tank and began filling. "That's the smart thing to do."

Glancing over his shoulder, I saw that the bed of his pickup was empty. "What happened to all the scrap metal you had?"

He shrugged. "Sold it up in Lafayette." His eyes glittered slyly. "Not bad money. Folks around here, they is always throwing away iron and aluminum. Been doing it forever."

"You've lived out on the river all your life, huh?"

He cut his eyes in my direction. They were bright and perceptive. "Over eighty years now."

"You know the Naquins?"

A quizzical frown knit his brow. "Clerville and his brood? Son, I know everybody in this here parish."

I glanced at the convenience store. "Well, if you have a little time, I'll buy you some coffee. I got a couple questions bothering me."

He cackled. "That's the one thing I got plenty of, time."

Chapter Six

We slid into a booth next to a plate-glass window overlooking the front drive. Rouly hadn't lied when he said he knew everyone. Not a soul passed who didn't speak, nod, or grunt to him. He sipped his coffee. "Now, what was it you had on your mind, son?"

"Looking to find out anything you can tell me about the Naquins upriver from here."

"What do you want to know?"

"They lived here all their lives?"

"And then some. They is what you call Chitimacha Indians. They was living here even before our folks come in from Nova Scotia. Not many of them be left, maybe a hundred or so." He paused. "Why you be asking?"

That explained the Naquins' straight black hair instead of the curly locks of the Cajun. "I met them today. I'm from up around Church Point, but I couldn't understand some of their words. They were a little different from the Cajun French I grew up with."

Cupping his coffee in two hands, he leaned forward on his elbows and sipped at the steaming liquid. "That's the Indian in them." He paused and then added, "I remember when Clerville was born. His daddy, Emile, he throw a big *fais-do-do,* with barbecue *cochon.* We be eating hog and dancing for three days."

His words brought my childhood rushing back. I always looked forward to the *fais-do-dos* and the barbecued *cochon.* Parents gathered in the living room and kitchen, put the kids to sleep in another room, and danced the night away.

The older kids, like me, usually spent the night in the barn telling ghost stories and playing games such as *Cache, cache la bague*, which was "hide a ring," where players in a circle pass a ring from one to the other behind their backs, and then on the command, one must guess who holds the ring. Then there was *Petit mouton, la queue coupee,* "little sheep with a cut tail," where a player with a handkerchief walks around the circle and drops it behind someone, who then picks it up and tries to tag the other player.

Rouly pulled out a pack of Lucky Strikes and fished one from the package. He held the cigarette between tobacco-stained fingers and looked up at me. "They mighty fine folks, living the life the old ones lived. 'Course, that life, like the one me, I got, is disappearing like the red wolf, the oysters, and miles and miles of wetlands. Why, I can remember when the river was lined with shacks. Then—" He glanced at the NO SMOKING sign and snorted. "The *riche blanc gens,* the rich white people, they come in, and all change." He touched a match to his cigarette. "The Naquins, they good people."

"Valsin looks to be the oldest."

Rouly replied, "That he be. That one, he know the swamps even better than me. Between that one and his alligators, and the brothers with their shrimp and crabs, the eating houses around Priouxville and Charenton, they take all the boys can bring in."

"Alligators? But isn't there a season on them?"

Rouly cackled. "The Federal and state boys, they learn long ago not to go in the swamp with Valsin."

Pondering his reply, I found myself glad Valsin liked me. "Who owned the house before my friend bought it?"

He cocked his head to one side and looked at me curiously. "He dead now. Name be Guzik, Harry Guzik. He own the Sparkle Paradise north of Priouxville."

I remembered seeing the Sparkle, a fairly modern nightclub featuring a restaurant, dancing, and slots. "When did he die?"

Rouly pursed his wrinkled lips. "Let me see now." He ran his bony fingers under his straw hat to scratch his head. "Seems like sometime around January or February. The weather, it be mighty cold, best I remember."

January or February? But Jack had signed the papers in March. Probably, I told myself, the executor consummated the matter for Guzik's estate.

I had a feeling I could trust old Rouly, more or less. After all, I told myself, if rumors of diamonds on Jack's property had been circulating, the old Cajun would have heard of them, and he had more than enough time all by his lonesome to prowl the grounds.

He pushed his empty cup aside and started to rise.

"One other question, Mr. Rouly."

He paused halfway up, then sat back down. *"Oui."*

There had been a steady ebb and flow of customers in the Stop N Shop. So, lowering my voice, I leaned forward. "Have you ever heard any talk about diamonds on the place?"

I thought the question might surprise him, at least take him aback, but I was the one surprised when he shrugged and replied as casually as if I'd asked for a drink of water, *"Oui.* But I never find any. Me, I finally come to believe old Theriot, he don't hide the diamonds there."

I blinked once or twice, not certain I'd heard him right. "You mean, you've looked for them?"

Without a trace of embarrassment, he replied, *"Oui."*

"Didn't the owners protest?"

He winked, slyly. "I wait till they be gone." His gall amused me. He continued, "At first, me, I don't believe it that much. But a few years ago, some of the diamonds show up, they say. I don't know for sure, but that be what I hear. So, I look. I don't find them. Now—" He shrugged. "There are those who still come to look. Strangers. Nosy ones."

"You mentioned Theriot. Who's he?"

"Al Theriot. He own car lot north of Priouxville before he die. He the one they say pulled the diamond job. He die in prison, up to Winn Parish. He was killed in a riot." He leaned forward and dropped his voice to a whisper. "They say the Mafia, it kill him and them what worked with him." He paused, then added, "Kind of like a lesson to them what butts into Mafia business." He shrugged. "That just be what I hear."

I remembered the two goons from the previous day. "Do you know who owns the Golden Crystal Casino?"

He seemed to consider the question. "I not be sure, but I think the name be O'Donnell. Talk was that he took over when his uncle—a Mafia one named Strollo—died. The uncle, he part of the Chicago mob, so they say. The sheriff, he can tell you."

"How long has the rumor of the diamonds been around?"

He shrugged. "Ever since the robbery," he replied, his tone suggesting such knowledge was common lore hereabouts. "That be, let me see, back in '96. The Eloi Saint Julian Jewelers in New Orleans. Eight million."

I eyed him suspiciously. "In '96? That's thirteen years ago. How can you remember the details after all these years?"

"My nephew, Sostene, he work at the jewelers. That one, he tell us all about the robbery. They put his picture in the paper. Me, I have it framed on my wall. Sostene, he be the son of my sister, Totilde."

As I watched old man Rouly drive away, I reminded myself not to take all he said as gospel. I'd lived among the old-timers and those on the outskirts of our society long enough to know they usually said just enough to keep the listener happy, but there was no way he would reveal any secrets of his own people. Valsin might have been a hatchet killer, but old Rouly would never have let a word of it roll off his dried-up lips even if he thought he could benefit from the disclosure.

My next stop was the Golden Crystal Casino. I didn't fool myself that deacons of the local Baptist church operated the casino and track. Though over the last couple of decades the mob had lost some of its power and influence, especially among the younger generations, the desire for easy money is just as much a driving force today as back in the days of Abe Bernstein and his Purple Gang in Detroit.

I decided I needed an ace in the hole, so I called Danny O'Banion in Austin. Danny and I have a history that goes back to the eleventh grade, where we managed to get into a few scrapes together. He dropped out in the twelfth grade, and we went our separate ways, me into teaching, and him into the mob.

A few years back, I'd endeared myself to his superiors by saving them a few million bucks on a stock market rip-off. One thing I quickly learned about them, they didn't forget their friends, or their enemies.

While it isn't something I'd particularly want engraved on my tombstone, I am one of the few Joe Six-Packs who can get through to Danny on the phone.

When he picked up, we chitchatted for a few moments, arranged a dinner at the County Line Barbecue out on Bee Tree Road west of Austin, and then got down to business.

I told him about the assault on Jack, the rumor of the diamonds, and the name of the jewelers, Eloi Saint Julian Jewelers over in New Orleans. "That was back in '96."

He whistled softly. "When you step into a pile of trouble, you make sure it's a big pile, don't you?"

Puzzled, I replied, "What do you mean?"

"If it's what I think it is, I've heard about it. You and me were still making our bones when it happened."

"The heist?"

"Yeah. Word back then was that Joe Vasco had just taken over New Orleans after Mike Pisano croaked. Heart attack. The heist took place on his turf. He sent his soldiers out looking for the jokers who pulled it off."

"Did he find them?"

"Yeah. They were amateurs. Can you believe it? Three stupid amateurs pulled off an eight-million-dollar heist right under Joe Vasco's nose. Naturally, Joe went after them, but the cops got the ringleader first. The others were carried out of prison in coffins."

"What about the jewels?"

"No trace. I don't know if it's true or not, but supposedly Vasco got in touch with his contacts at Winn Correctional facility in an effort to find out what that yokel did with the jewels." He paused. "What are you asking all this for?"

I explained what I knew. "So now, I'm heading out to the

casino to find out who the two goons are. I was hoping you knew the owner, a guy named Anthony O'Donnell."

Danny paused a moment. "Name's not familiar, but if he's running the casino, you can bet Joe Vasco gets his share."

I knew exactly what he meant, but I vocalized it anyway. "In other words, the only reason he's there is because Vasco okays him."

"In Louisiana, that's the name of the game, Tony boy."

Chapter Seven

The imposing façade of glass and brick of the Golden Crystal Casino was ablaze. At either end of the four-story building, a golden bottle tilted, poured a drink into a golden martini glass, and then a golden woman drank the martini.

The regular parking lot was full, as was the valet parking. I couldn't help noticing that a third of the vehicles were from Texas. It is a fact that as you draw closer to the Texas border, the proportion of Texas plates in casino parking lots burgeons to almost 90 percent.

Eight double glass doors welcomed me. The casino's lobby was as wide as a football field. Off to the left was the hotel lobby; on the other side were the slots; beyond them, doors opened to the racetrack. Farther down the lobby were two bars with TVs blaring. Flights of stairs and escalators led to the second floor and the gaming tables.

To the left of the front desk, doors opened to a dining patio, which was over half full at this time of day. I paused at the top of the stairs just outside the door, looking around to orient myself. I spotted the marina off to my left.

I took the flight of stairs down to the docks. Boisterous shouts came from the saloons of several of the larger boats—*yachts* would be a more appropriate designation. I made my way along the main pier to the office next to the metal boat shed.

I did a double take. The office was twice the size of my apartment back on Payton-Gin Road in Austin. At the desk near the door sat an elderly man wearing a brown uniform with GOLDEN CRYSTAL CASINO embroidered over one pocket, and his name,

WALTER, over the other. A full cup of coffee sat in front of him. At the end of the room, four plush leather couches sat before a flat-screen TV on the wall. Three pool tables ran along the fourth wall, two of them occupied. One of the players was bald. He wore a striped polo shirt.

One of the men running from Jack's house was bald, I thought.

The guard looked up. "Yes, sir. What can I do for you?"

"Just a question. That yellow Stratos in the boat shed. Can you tell me who owns it? I saw it this morning, and I'd like to make the owner an offer."

A pool player looked around and growled, "It ain't for sale, pal."

Thickly built, he appeared to be in his late forties, with curly black hair. He had all the accoutrements of an ex-boxer: broken nose, scars over his eyebrows, knotty knuckles, and a crooked sneer that suggested he lived in two worlds, this one, and one of his own, created by too many encounters in the boxing ring.

"You the owner?"

He waved the pool cue threateningly. "No. But like I say, it ain't for sale." He slapped the butt of the cue stick into one of his meaty hands. He leered at his pool partner, a long-haired man who looked Native American.

I turned back to the guard. "I'd like for the owner tell me it isn't for sale."

The ex-pug stepped forward and grabbed my shoulder to spin me around. With a curse, he yelled, "I said that—"

I grabbed the hot coffee and threw it into his face.

He screamed and grabbed at his face.

I yanked the cue stick from his grasp and broke it over his head. He dropped without a sound. I glared at the other three. The Indian took a step. With the butt of the cue stick, I gestured for him to take another step. "You want some?"

The bald-headed pool player at his side growled, "Back away, Mule."

The dark-complexioned man stopped and looked around at his friends. He studied them for a moment and then looked around at me. After a few moments, he took a step backward. I turned to the guard. "Now, are you going to tell me, or do you want some of it?"

He swallowed hard. "Mr. O'Donnell. Anthony O'Donnell. He owns it."

"Where is he?"

"His . . . his office. Fourth floor."

"Thanks." I tossed the broken cue stick onto his desk and gestured to the unconscious Neanderthal on the floor. "If he wants me when he wakes up, tell him to get in touch with Sheriff Thertule Lacoutrue. He knows I'm here." It was a lie, but by the time the truth was discovered, if ever, I'd be long gone.

I stepped into the elevator and punched the fourth-floor button. When the doors opened, two stone-faced goons in Jay Kos suits stood staring at me. One of them growled, "You're on the wrong floor, friend."

"If this is where O'Donnell has his office, I'm not."

Neither caveman replied. Maybe those six words were all they were programmed to speak.

Behind them the door opened, and another button man stuck his head out. "Let him in."

The two monoliths stepped aside, and I crossed the lobby to the open door. The smaller man rolled his shoulders and peered up at me. "You the one Lacoutrue sent?"

"Lacoutrue didn't send me. I came on my own." I shifted my gaze to a tanned blond neatly attired in a beige suit behind a large desk. He would have looked more at home on a California movie set than in a Louisiana casino.

I glanced around the spacious office. The dapper man at the desk rose. His coiffed hair remained rigid. I couldn't help wondering how much hair spray he used. His tone was cool, his manner aloof, even wary. "I haven't had the pleasure, Mr.—"

I crossed the room to his desk, my feet sinking into the plush carpet. "Boudreaux. And you must be Anthony O'Donnell." Neither of us extended a hand.

He glanced at my empty hands and remarked, "Did you lose the cue stick?"

Somewhat surprised at his smooth manner, I replied, "His manners were lacking. Anyone can see yours aren't."

"For that, I thank you." He pointed a slender, almost delicate finger at a tray of crystal carafes. "Something to drink? Bourbon, vodka, rum?"

"No, thanks, Mr. O'Donnell. I'm here on business, and I hope you can help me out. Joe Vasco seems to think you can." Which was a bald-faced lie, but I had learned long ago that sometimes tossing names around like a shotgun blast can effect results that otherwise might never be gained.

To say the name impressed him was as much an understatement as saying the Mississippi River was nothing more than a dry-weather creek. Immediately, his manner grew warm, his tone amiable. "Please, have a seat. Tell me what assistance I can offer."

Sliding into a leather chair, I recounted the events of the last few days, starting with the assault on Jack and ending with my arrival at Jack's house and spotting the two goons jump into the yellow Stratos and race away. "The boat is moored down in your boat shed, Mr. O'Donnell. I can't identify the two. One was bald, but that is hardly a definitive means to describe him."

He laughed softly. "I understand that, but I assure you, Mr. Boudreaux, none of my employees would have any reason to be prowling around your friend's home."

"All I can tell you is I saw two men run down the stairs, jump into the Stratos, and take off. One was bald. And the boat is in your boat shed."

He eyed me shrewdly. "If you don't mind telling me, how do you know it's the same boat? Stratos is a common brand around here."

"Maybe so, but how many of them are yellow and have a ten-inch scar on the port side of the transom?"

He hesitated, his light gray eyes lowering their gaze to the desk as he tried to figure out how to respond. A faint smile curled his lips. "Very few, I should say."

"That's what I figured."

O'Donnell paused, studying me. "This bald-headed man—how old would you say he was?"

"Hard to say. He wasn't exactly standing still, but he wasn't young. I'd guess over forty."

He considered my information. "I see. Just a moment." He leaned forward and punched a button on his telephone. A deferential voice answered. "Jolene, send Carl up to see me, immediately." He punched off and leaned back in his plush leather swivel chair. With an ingratiating smile, he said, "He'll be right up. In the meantime, are you sure you wouldn't care for some refreshment?"

"Positive." I glanced around his office. "This is a nice place you have here." I looked back at him, a faint smile on my lips. "You must be pretty well connected to warrant such a job."

A flicker of anger clouded his dark eyes for a moment. "Since you know Vasco, you know how the system works. My uncle, Big Tim Strollo, financed the casino. He and Vasco had an agreement. After Tim passed away, Mr. Vasco and I honored the previous agreement."

What O'Donnell meant was that Vasco received a slice of the profits—not as much if he'd put up the financing, but in all probability more than three dozen hardworking Louisiana shrimpers made in a year. "Well, from what I saw, business is good."

He smiled in reply.

A knock at the door interrupted us. O'Donnell called out, "Come in, Carl."

The door opened, and the bald man in the striped polo shirt stepped inside. In a deferential voice, he said, "You wanted to see me, Mr. O'Donnell?"

"How long have we been together, Carl?"

The soldier shrugged his shoulders. "A long time, Mr. O'Donnell. Close to fifteen years." He cut his eyes nervously at me, then slid his gaze back to O'Donnell.

Expansively, O'Donnell replied, "Fifteen good years, and I've always been able to trust you. Isn't that right, Carl?"

"Yes, sir, Mr. O'Donnell."

"So I want you to tell me the truth, Carl."

A sheen of perspiration glinted on his bald pate. "Anything, Mr. O'Donnell."

O'Donnell explained, "This gentleman says yesterday, he saw two men running away from his friends' house down on the bayou. They got away in a yellow boat, which happens to be the Stratos in the boathouse." He paused. "What do you know about it?"

His wide eyes bouncing between O'Donnell and me like a Ping-Pong ball, Carl dragged the tip of his tongue over his lips. Taking a deep breath, he dropped his gaze to the floor. "That was me, Mr. O'Donnell."

With a merry twinkle in his eyes, O'Donnell winked at me. "Who was with you, Carl?"

His eyes still glued to the floor, he replied, "Patsy."

"Where is he?"

Carl lifted his head. "Down at the marina nursing the headache this guy gave him."

"Any others? Mule? Bobo?"

"No, sir. Just Patsy and me."

"I see. Why did you and Patsy go there?"

Carl chewed on his lips as if he were embarrassed to reply.

"I'm waiting, Carl, and you know I don't like to wait."

"The jewels, Mr. O'Donnell. Patsy and me had been hearing the rumors of loot from some diamond heist was hidden down there. We figured to prowl around. There ain't been nobody living down there."

The twinkle faded from O'Donnell's eyes. "This gentleman also said the owner of the house was worked over the night before. You know anything about it?"

The middle-aged button man shook his head emphatically. "No, sir."

"Was yesterday your only time there?"

Carl swallowed hard. "No, sir. Two more times. That's all. We never seen anybody there." He looked up at his boss. "That's the truth. I wouldn't lie to you. We didn't work nobody over down there."

Three times. That matched what Valsin had said.

O'Donnell snorted. "I hope not, Carl." His face grew hard. "That's a big swamp out there. You understand?"

Carl croaked, "Yes, sir."

"Good." O'Donnell waved his hand, dismissing the man. "Tell Patsy what I said."

"Yes, sir, I will," Carl replied, backing away to the door. "Thank you, Mr. O'Donnell. Thank you."

After the door closed behind O'Donnell's soldier, the dapper casino owner gave a half laugh. "They won't bother you again, Mr. Boudreaux." He paused. "I'm sorry I couldn't help you find those who assaulted your friend, but I have no doubt Carl told us the truth."

Well aware of the unwavering loyalty mob soldiers had for their boss, I knew O'Donnell was right. I scooted forward in my chair. "Naturally, I'd like to get my hands on those who worked over my friend, but to be honest, you and I both know I'll probably never find them."

While his face remained impassive, a glint of triumph filled his eyes. "You're probably right." He rocked back and forth in his chair a couple of times. "I'd heard the same rumors—about the jewels, I mean. That was years ago, and from what I heard, all those who took part are dead."

I played dumb, thinking I might pick up some more information. "I hadn't heard anything about that."

"My uncle, Big Tim Strollo, told me. From what he said, Vasco went after the three in prison. Tim didn't go into any detail, only that it didn't pay to buck Joe Vasco."

"But the diamonds have never been found?"

He smiled faintly. "Hard to say. A few years ago, rumors surfaced that some had been. Who knows? Not me. Personally, I think it's like all the old stories about old-timers hiding money in glass jars and that sort of thing. If the truth were known, the entire haul has probably been spread all over the world by now. One thing's for certain, I'm not going to worry about them." He gestured to his surroundings. "With all due respect to my patrons, this place is a diamond mine in its own right."

Chapter Eight

Back in my pickup, I stared out the window at the casino. O'Donnell had sounded sincere. To be honest, I couldn't see the logic of someone in his position chasing after a will-o'-the-wisp or the *feu follet* for diamonds that would bring nothing but grief.

Of course, I reminded myself, he might believe retrieving the diamonds would further ingratiate himself to Joe Vasco, the New Orleans mob leader.

One discomforting aspect of the PI life is that you tend to lean toward cynicism. The mantra of Al Grogan, our resident Sherlock Holmes at Blevins' Security, was "believe nothing."

That proved to be a most valuable piece of advice, often permitting me to perceive alternative agendas in running down the solution in various cases.

Another discomforting aspect of the job is the cold reality that in many instances, assaults, robberies, and other crimes go unpunished, the guilty managing to slither away to find other victims.

If someone had asked me at that moment if I believed I would find those who jumped Jack, I would have said no.

By the time I parked under the carport, the moon had risen, lighting the yard and walkways in eerie relief. One thing every Louisianan knows is that if you walk the shores of a bayou at night, you carry a flashlight and a big stick, because somewhere along the way you're going to run into a tangle of snakes holding a family reunion.

When Diane and I left that afternoon, we'd failed to leave a light burning, so the house was dark. I opened the door and felt along the wall for a switch.

When I found one, light flooded the living room, and I almost jumped out of my skin.

Coiled on the carpet not six feet away was a black snake. Instinctively I jumped back onto the porch and slammed the screen in front of me. When I did, the snake uncoiled and slithered across the room.

To my relief, I spotted the red blotches on its black scales and realized it was only a mud snake, not the dreaded cottonmouth. Cottonmouths—or water moccasins, as they're sometimes called—are belligerent and aggressive. While most snakes retreat at human approach, the cottonmouth obstinately refuses to move, his musky odor permeating the air around him, and his sullen attitude daring anyone to take a single step closer.

Still, a mud snake will bite if cornered, and this one was at least five feet long, going on fifty as far as I was concerned. He glided under the couch.

I rolled my eyes. Diane would have a heart attack if she walked in and found a snake staring up at her. I couldn't suppress a chuckle. If she were to see one, she'd climb the walls and perch on the chandelier.

Slipping inside, I kept my eyes on the couch while I hastily closed all the doors leading from the living area and jammed towels under them, sealing off the front room from the rest of the house.

Having grown up in the country in my grandparents' old house, we'd had more than one snake explore the premises. I'll never forget when I was about five or six, I rose during the night and padded to the bathroom. Grand-mère Ola always kept a small light on in the kitchen. As I passed the kitchen door, I glanced inside. A snake slithering across the linoleum floor paused, looked at me, and then continued casually on his way.

Next morning, I told Mamère. She shrugged it off. "Oh, that be Jean. He been here since before you was born. He help keep the rats down." She winked at me. "He big help around here, not like some little *garçons,* me, I know."

I knew she meant me, but I didn't know she was teasing.

That was the last time I saw Jean, but a few months later, Mamère told me she had found Jean dead and tossed him to the hogs. "That what happens to all *mauvais petit garçons.*"

Remembering she had said Jean was more help to her than me, and that I was sometimes a "bad little boy," I had nightmares for a week. If she would throw *him* to the hogs, what would she do with me? For the next couple of months, I watched her warily and made it a point to stay away from the hog pens.

Somehow, I didn't think Diane would be quite as casual about the presence of a snake in her house, so I planned to fall back on a surefire method of ridding the area of snakes.

Rummaging through her kitchen spices, I found a bottle of cloves. I crushed the small cloves and then boiled them in water. The result was a poor substitute for clove oil, for which Grand-mère Ola had had myriad uses, even my acne and occasional warts.

After the water boiled down to a few ounces, I dumped the contents from a plastic bottle of Formula 409 cleaner I found under the sink and poured my solution of clove syrup into it. I put some on my finger and tasted it. I could taste the clove, although it was much weaker than the real stuff.

I crossed my fingers and went back into the living room. I propped open the front storm door, and then, with the handle of a broom, raised the skirt on the bottom of the couch and fired half a dozen squirts under it before jumping back.

The mud snake shot out one end of the couch and tried to climb the wall. He fell back and headed my way. Stumbling backward, I squirted again and yelled, "Hah!" He whipped around and headed back toward the door. Ten seconds later, he disappeared into the night.

I soaked the porch with my solution of clove. Finally, I closed the door and relaxed on the couch. And then it hit me. How did the mud snake get inside? If it had been my grandparents' old home, it would be a moot question. That house was full of holes, but this one?

I glanced around the living room. With the windows closed and the doors shut, there was no way for a snake to slither in. Besides, I remembered Jack saying they'd had the place sprayed with snake repellent.

Digging out a flashlight, I turned on the porch lights and the lights below. Downstairs, I searched the storage rooms as well as the floor joists, which I discovered the contractors had completely closed in, leaving only tightly sealed hatches to access various components needing service.

When I went back upstairs, the overpowering aroma of clove smacked me in the face. I threw open the windows to air out the house, wondering just how I would explain the smell to Diane.

Later, after I turned off the lights, I stood staring out the storm door into the pitch-black swamp. No question. My mud snake had had help getting in.

But how, and why?

Obviously, someone wants to get rid of Jack and Diane.

And the reason why was a chump guess. The diamonds!

The next several minutes, I sorted through the tangle of events of the last couple of days, trying to put my thoughts into order, if possible.

The scenario was simple. Someone wanted the diamonds, and that someone figured the gems were on the premises. If they could run Jack and Diane off, they could tear the place apart without any interference.

I glanced out the window. As fanciful as it seemed, I had the feeling the diamonds were close.

Of course, I reminded myself, I might be reaching too far, trying to snatch at a possibility that never existed, but the snake in the living room added enough to the conundrum to convince me there was some substance to my tenuous theory.

I flipped on the kitchen light. Sitting at the snack bar that divided the kitchen from the dining area, I jotted down my ideas. The mastermind of the '96 heist was Al Theriot, who owned a car dealership north of town. He was sent to Winn Correctional, where he was killed in a riot in '97. I grinned. *Killed?* Not quite. *Assassinated* was a much more apropos explanation.

According to O'banion, Theriot had had two accomplices, both sent to prison and each leaving the slammer in a coffin. Again, the handiwork of Joe Vasco.

Just recently, L. Q. Benoit, an ex-con fresh out of Winn, was found dead on the outskirts of Priouxville. According to old Rouly, it was the handiwork of the mythical loup-garou, a shape-changer that could take on the form of either human or animal. That was a pile of nonsense. The old man was murdered, and not by any specter.

I paused, studying the words before me, wondering if there were a connection. What if Benoit had somehow learned of the hidden diamonds? I made a note to see if Sheriff Lacoutrue could learn the name of Benoit's cell mates up at Winn.

For the next few minutes, I toyed with the possibility of some sort of tie-in between Benoit and Anthony O'Donnell. I had no doubt the casino owner could have lied about the diamonds. Who wouldn't? Of course, I reminded myself, while such a possibility existed, it was still quite a stretch.

Glancing back over my notes, I saw again that the robbery was thirteen years old. Almost ancient history by today's standards, but apparently someone had decided to delve back into the past. After all, I told myself, eight million was mighty enticing, and in today's market, given its volatility, the eight could be worth as much as from twelve to twenty.

Having exhausted my meager supply of ideas, I tossed my pencil onto the notepad and leaned back. Tomorrow morning after I visited the hospital, I'd head for the newspaper office.

I rose and stretched. I glanced out the window one last time and froze as flickering lights played through the swamp. I hurried to the front window, watching the light move through the trees and then, in the blink of an eye, vanish.

When I awoke the next morning, the pungent smell of clove still hung in the air, and I still hadn't come up with a good lie for Diane to explain the odor. I couldn't tell her the truth. She'd never set foot in the house again.

Reluctantly, I closed all the windows and locked them before I left. I didn't want any more surprises waiting. The smell of clove would be bad enough.

Chapter Nine

Jack was healing quickly. He still looked like death, but the sparkle had returned to his eyes. I glanced at Diane sitting beside his bed. She looked as if she could use a long rest as well.

"The doctor just left," she said. "He says Jack's doing better than he expected."

"That's good news. He say how long he's going to keep you in here?" I asked Jack.

"Not much longer," he muttered through clenched teeth. "Nothing else they can do for the arm. I'm hoping tomorrow."

Diane gave him a wan smile. She was exhausted. The dark circles under her eyes spoke volumes. "We don't want to rush anything, Jack."

He winked at me. "You hear that? She's a jewel, huh?"

"Yeah. She's a jewel."

"Don't worry," he told her. "I'll do whatever the doc says. Now, you need to go home and get some rest." He looked back up at me. "Take care of her, okay?"

I cursed to myself. I'd planned on stopping by the sheriff's office as well as the local newspaper. Now I was going to be hamstrung for the rest of the day taking care of my ex-wife. "Sure, Jack. You just take it easy."

Diane slid behind the wheel of her Cadillac. She looked at me before closing the door. "I need to stop at the market first. I'll be right along."

"No problem," I replied, almost gleefully. "I've got a couple of stops to make myself."

She forced a weary smile. "I'll see you out at the house."

Sheriff Lacoutrue looked up when I opened the door. "Morning."

"Good morning, Sheriff. Looks like a hot day. Probably thunderstorms later."

At a desk against the wall, a second officer looked around. Lacoutrue said, "That be my deputy, Paul Thibodeaux."

I smiled. "Morning."

Thibodeaux was a few inches shorter than the sheriff but just as thin. He studied me for a moment and then dipped his head. "Good morning."

Lacoutrue leaned back in his chair. "Well, Mr. Boudreaux. How be your friend?"

"Good. Probably come home in a few days."

He pursed his lips. "That sound good."

"Any luck in running down who might have jumped him?"

"*Mais non,* no luck, but me, I do talk to LeBlanc. He say to tell you hello."

"He's a good man," I replied.

"*Oui.*"

I grew serious. "Sheriff, when I was last here, you mentioned a murder a couple of weeks back. Was that the old boy named Benoit?"

"How you know?"

"I ran into an old gentleman named Rouly."

Lacoutrue chuckled. "Old Rouly. He be the local scrap man. That one, he know everything what go on in this parish."

"Well, he said Benoit had just gotten out of Winn Correctional."

He frowned. "That what they say. He was supposed to see me about the parole, but he never come by. Why you want to know?"

That was the one question I was hoping he wouldn't ask. In my business, convincing lies sometimes are an asset, but for the life of me, I couldn't come up with one that made any sense. I decided to take a drastic step and tell him the truth. "I know this is probably going to sound idiotic to you, Sheriff, but—" I hesitated.

He leaned back in his chair, eyeing me suspiciously. "But what?"

I gestured to the chair in front of his desk. "May I sit?"

"Sure. Take a load off. Me, I'm interested in what you got to say."

"After I left you the day before yesterday, I ran into Mr. Rouly down the road." Over the next few minutes, I sketched out all that had taken place since, up through the snake in the house the previous night.

"So," I concluded, "Al Theriot owned the house at the time he masterminded the robbery."

The sheriff shook his head. "*Mais non.* He sell to Ramsey, the superintendent, before he rob the jewelry store."

I grimaced. That piece of information put a little crimp in my theory. "If he didn't own it, then why is there so much talk about the diamonds being at his old place?"

Lacoutrue shrugged. "Me, I got no idea, but that's the talk, and it don't go away."

I pondered the new information. "Okay. If that's the talk, then it makes no difference. Like I was saying, Theriot and his two accomplices died in prison. And since the jewels are still missing—"

He stopped me. "Maybe not all."

"Yeah. I heard some surfaced a few years back. Now the two down at the casino, Carl and Patsy, admitted looking for the diamonds at the house. Rouly has searched everywhere down there by his own admission."

"So, what you got in mind?" The sheriff rocked forward in his chair.

"I want to see if I can find the diamonds or at least what happened to them."

"Why?"

I pursed my lips while I formed my response. "The diamonds and the assault on my friend are related." I decided to be perfectly honest with Lacoutrue. "According to Jack, one of the goons who jumped him demanded to know the whereabouts of the diamonds. Proof enough that's what they were looking for, right?"

"Just what you got in mind?" he asked again.

I suppressed a smile. "All right, maybe I'm reaching, but I've got to have a starting place. It strikes me as curious that an ex-con found beaten to death was paroled from the same prison where Theriot and his accomplices served their time. Makes me wonder if the two are somehow connected. I'd like to know who Benoit's cell mates were at Winn."

"What good will that do?"

"I don't know." I shrugged. "What if . . . what if Benoit somehow got on to where the jewels were hidden? What if he planned to get them?" I shook my head. "I might just be grabbing at air, but at least it's someplace to start."

"So you think," he began, "that them what killed Benoit might be the ones what whipped up your friend?"

"It's possible," I replied. "Can you find out who his cell mates were?"

Sheriff Lacoutrue didn't answer for several moments. Finally, he replied, "*Oui,* I can do that for you."

"Great. How long do you figure it'll take?"

He shook his head. "Not long. Me, I'll get Thibodeaux here to call up there this morning."

Thibodeaux nodded.

I had more questions, most of which the sheriff could probably have answered, but I was reluctant to keep asking them. At any time he could have figured I was getting too nosy or butting into his business and insisted I steer clear of the whole matter. "Thanks, Sheriff."

After leaving the sheriff's office, I headed for the local newspaper, the *Priouxville Bayou News.* All I wanted was a list of those who had owned the house. I wasn't sure what good it would do, but at least it gave me some names to investigate.

I didn't plan on mentioning the diamonds, for, given the dynamics of small towns, were I to mention the jewels, everyone in town would know before I left the office.

Well, perhaps not that quickly, but within five minutes for sure. *On the other hand, Tony, you dummy,* I told myself, *probably everybody in town already knows more about them than you.*

Like all small-town papers, the *Bayou*'s archives left a great deal to be desired, but the longtime editor and owner, seventy-six-year-old Louis Brasseaux and his ace reporter, sixty-three-year-old Emerente Landry, both knew even more about the community than old Rouly, saving me a world of digging through dusty files. Emerente, like most Cajun women, wore her hair swept up on her head in a bouffant and not a strand out of place.

Between the two of them, over a pot of coffee, half a dozen chocolate-covered éclairs, and several heated exchanges on the questionable deterioration of each other's memory, I learned that the previous owner, Harry Guzik, who owned the Sparkle Paradise nightclub north of town, was murdered in July 2008.

The announcement got my attention. Had he been involved with the diamonds? What other explanation for his murder? "July, huh? I thought it was during colder weather, winter or so."

The two gazed, unseeing, at each other. Brasseaux pursed his wrinkled lips. "No. July. I remember that well."

Rouly had said the winter, but now the editor claimed six months earlier. I shrugged the discrepancy off. "So, during the summer, huh? That's when he was killed?"

Emerente interrupted. "Some say that one, he kill himself. So there," she added, as if punctuating her remark with an exclamation point.

Brasseaux snorted. "That be impossible. How that one, he shoot himself in the back of the head?" He snorted again. "Nope. That be a mob hit." He glared at Emerente.

After they settled that disagreement, I learned that Guzik had purchased the home from Big Tim Strollo, who had owned it for five or six years.

Before Strollo, retired superintendent Jimmy Ramsey owned the house for a few years. He had been living in a leased cabin down the bayou, but when Theriot, running into financial problems, put his place up for sale, Ramsey bought it.

The old editor explained that Theriot's father, Alexandre, had bought the house from the Priouxes, and after he died, young Al later moved the house a hundred feet to a crest well above the thousand-year flood level and completely remodeled it, keeping, however, as much of the cypress logs as possible, especially the front stairs and their unique railings and balusters.

"They are beautiful," Emerente said. "Have you ever looked at them, really looked at them?"

Sheepishly, I shrugged. I'd looked at them enough not to like them. "Not really."

"Do. On the side of the handrails and balusters are hand-carved fleurs-de-lis." She shook her head. "Simply magnificent," she gushed.

I wasn't about to fall into a discussion about the cypress railings and balusters. Personally, regardless of the fleur-de-lis carvings, I thought they were as out of place on the house as a wart on a beautiful woman's nose.

Brasseaux grunted and ran his hand through his long white hair. "That Theriot, me, I never see no one so picky about the way that house be built."

Emerente snorted. "That one, he should have been more particular about robbing that jewelry store over in New Orleans with the Judice brothers." She gave her head an emphatic shake.

Putting on what I hoped was an expression of naivety, I replied, "Jewel robbery? I hadn't heard that."

"*Oui*. It happen back in '96. That why Theriot, he go to prison." Smugly, she looked around at Brasseaux.

The old editor glared at her and then added, "Theriot, he plan the job with C. K. and Donat Judice, so say Lacoutrue." He grinned smugly at Emerente.

Her eyes narrowed. I had the feeling she was not to be out-done by her boss. "What you mean, 'so say Lacoutrue'? That sheriff, he dumber than a snake. It be Thibodeaux what run them down, but it not be the boys who plan the job. It be Theriot. The boys, they just be with him. That's why the law, Lacoutrue, he don't catch them at first."

Brasseaux wagged a finger at her. "You forget to say that some of the jewels show up eight years later."

She grimaced, as if chiding herself for forgetting such a juicy piece of gossip. "That be right," she replied. "From what we hear,

the jewels was found in a pawnshop up in Alexandria. The owners over in New Orleans still have a reward up for the rest of the
jewels." She looked at Brasseaux. "Me, I forget how much. You
remember?"

His bushy white eyebrows ran together when he furrowed his
brow in concentration. "Best I recollect, it was the Eloi Saint
Julian Jewelers, and they offered a 25 percent reward for the
jewels."

I whistled to myself. No wonder people had been searching
for the diamonds. Keeping an impassive face, I replied, "Any
luck?"

Emerente shook her head, her bouffant hairdo bobbing back
and forth. "No. Not counting those in Alexandria."

Brasseaux nodded to my empty coffee cup. "We got more."

I shook my head. "You mentioned they didn't catch the Judice boys until later. They didn't go to prison with Theriot?"

The old editor rolled his eyes. "It be several years before
Lacoutrue learn the Judice boys was with Theriot."

"Just before the statute of limitations run out," Emerente said,
punctuating her remark with a firm shake of her head.

Brasseaux grimaced at the interruption. "That be right."

Emerente continued, "Thibodeaux, he tell the sheriff. That's
how Lacoutrue know."

Brasseaux glared at her. "You want to tell this story?"

She glared back.

"All right, then," the old man continued. "By then Theriot was
dead, but the boys was sent to prison. That be about seven or
eight years ago. Donat, he die there. C. K., he was a mean one.
Tried to break out and got another ten years."

"He still there?"

Emerente poured another cup of coffee. "He be killed too, three
years ago. Riot." She shook her head. "That be terrible place."

I glanced down at my notes. "That's interesting. Now, this
Guzik—what can you tell me about him?"

Chapter Ten

Emerente shrugged. "That one, he keep to himself."

Louis nodded in agreement.

Patting the back of her hairdo, the Bayou's ace reporter continued, "When Guzik not at the nightclub, he be at his place on the bayou. Me, I never see him in Priouxville, not once in all that time." She looked around at her editor. "How long that be? Five or six years?"

Brasseaux grunted. "About that. He keep mighty close to himself. I hear the boys at the electric company say they never see no one at the house." He paused and shivered.

Emerente jumped back in. "Then one morning, the mailman, that be Prosper Esteve, he find Guzik floating under the bridge over Alligator Bayou. He managed to throw a rope over the body and drag it to shore."

Brasseaux clucked his tongue. "What be left of it." He leaped to his feet and wagged a wrinkled finger. "Me, I get you something." He rummaged through a file cabinet and moments later returned with a page of news copy. He handed it to me. "This tell you about Guzik," he said, pointing to the byline. "Emerente, she write this two days after his body, it be found. Good story," he added, winking at her.

She beamed.

I remained with the two chatterboxes another thirty minutes, managing to glean a few pieces of information that might prove to be stepping stones—to what, I wasn't sure.

Big Tim Strollo had died of a heart attack; Ramsey had moved out after suffering financial losses; Theriot died in prison, and

58

his partner, Oscar Mouton, continued running Bayou Country Motors; and the only remaining members of the Prioux family were in their nineties and lived at Priouxville Glen Care Center.

As I rose to leave, Brasseaux said, "I suppose you already met old Rouly out your way, huh?"

I laughed. "Yeah."

"That one, he be quite a character."

"I could tell. He even told me about one of your citizens, L. Q. Benoit, who was found dead. Claimed it was a loup-garou." I expected a smile from them, but both grew serious.

Emerente spoke up. "Me, I don't believe all that much in such stories, but there be two more what be killed like Benoit."

My own smile faded. "What's that?"

Brasseaux ran his wrinkled fingers through his full head of white hair. "*Oui,* Charley Primeaux and Dudley Vitale. They be found dead. Beat to death like Benoit."

A hint of fear glittered in Emerente's eyes. "There be tracks of the horse by them. Me, I know for sure they be by Dudley. I see them."

The old editor knit his brow. "Naturally, we all know there be no such thing as loup-garou, but the sheriff, he say the autopsies show they was beat to death. By a horse."

Emerente arched a pencil-darkened eyebrow. "You think what you want. Like I say, I see them tracks by Dudley, but then," she added, a hint of Old Country superstition in her voice, "the tracks, they disappear."

I frowned. "What do you mean, 'disappear'?"

She held up her arms in exclamation. "Disappear, vanish, go away." She explained, "Dudley, that one, he was found beside the dirt road to his shack. The tracks, they was all around him, and then they was no more. I look for them, but they be gone." She pointed to a spot on the floor. "They go down the road, and then," she said, pointing to another spot, "they not there. Only footprints made by a boot, the boot of that one who become the loup-garou." She jumped to her feet. "I show you." She rummaged through a file cabinet.

Brasseaux snorted and rolled his eyes. "Next thing that one be saying is that it was all voodoo. Marie Laveau reborn."

Emerente glanced over her shoulder, her eyes shooting daggers at him. "You don't know nothing, you foolish old man. Just you wait. Ah, here it be." She opened a folder and handed me two pictures. "This be what I talking about."

The first 8×10 glossy showed a series of horse tracks leading from a body in a ditch and ending abruptly in the middle of the dusty road, where a set of human footprints took over. The second was a close-up of one of the tracks.

I glanced at the second one and then looked again, realizing the one leg of the horseshoe's U was bent outward a couple of degrees.

She jabbed a finger at the first glossy and glared at Brasseaux. "Now, how you explain that, old man?"

Brasseaux just snorted. "Simple. The passing cars, they wipe the tracks out." He shook his shaggy head of white hair. "There be nothing supernatural about that."

She snorted. "You ain't worth talking to, you know?"

I pushed to my feet, figuring I'd leave before the two came to blows. "I appreciate the information."

She smiled at me. "Come back anytime. We open seven days a week. After church on Sundays."

Out in the pickup, I glanced at my notes, concentrating on the diamonds. Any of the names on my list could have discovered them. Unfortunately, three of them were dead. Shaking my head, I slipped the note cards into my shirt pocket and started the engine. I couldn't question dead men, but I could question those who knew them.

The sun baked down from directly overhead when I pulled under the carport and parked beside the Cadillac. I didn't even want to think about how the heat would have intensified the smell of clove.

I sighed with relief when I saw that the windows were thrown wide open. I rolled my eyes, knowing my ex-wife was waiting for an explanation—one that I still hadn't managed to fabricate.

I opened the storm door and winced as the odor of clove hit me. I called out, "Diane! It's me, Tony."

"Back here," she replied from the kitchen.

I looked past the snack bar but failed to see her. Then she poked her head from behind the open refrigerator door. "I was going to make a sandwich. Want one?"

"Sure," I replied.

Closing the door, she placed dressings and lunch meat on the table. She hadn't changed clothes from the day before. "What happened last night? The house reeks of clove." She crossed the kitchen and opened the breadbox. "Huh?"

Up to that second, I had no answer, and then a response just rolled off my lying lips. I touched a finger to my jaw. "I had a toothache. I had a bottle of clove oil, but I dropped it, and it broke. Sorry."

She smiled and slid in at the snack bar. "Accidents happen. Fix your sandwich however you want it," she added, pointing to the ingredients on the table.

We made idle chitchat over a light lunch, after which she announced that she planned to take a nap.

That was fine with me. I had work to do on my laptop, and I wasn't any too keen about anyone looking over my shoulder. Later that day after I dropped her off at the hospital, I planned to pay a visit to the Sparkle Paradise. Guzik was dead, but maybe I could learn a little about him. He had bought the house from Big Tim Strollo, an influential mobster. Maybe I was grasping at straws, but at the time, I had nothing better to grasp.

All I needed was to come up with an enticing offer so the new owners of the Sparkle might consider loosening their tongues.

Booting up, I went online using my mobile broadband network card and contacted Eddie Dyson, my savior more than once.

At one time, Eddie was known as Austin's resident stool pigeon. Since then, he had become a computer whiz and wildly successful entrepreneur.

Instead of sleazy bars, back alleys, and dirty money, he'd found his niche for snitching in the bright glow of computers and the comforting security of credit cards. Any information I couldn't find, he could. Personally, I figured he had hacked into some kind of national database. What kind, I had no idea, but he always came up with information, information that suggested his total disregard of the principles of the 1974 Privacy Act.

There were only two catches if you dealt with Eddie. First, you never asked him how he did it, and second, he only accepted VISA credit cards for payment.

I never asked Eddie why just VISA. Seems like any credit card would be sufficient, but considering the value of his service, I never posed the question. As far as I was concerned, if he wanted to be paid in Albanian leks or Angolan new kwanza, I'd load up a couple dozen bushels and send them to him.

He seldom failed me. That's why I didn't mind his prices, which bordered on the obscene.

In my e-mail, I requested information on the jewel heist as well as on each of the previous owners of the house. I wasn't sure if there were more that I needed or not. When I got that information, I'd see where I stood. As an afterthought, I asked for the cell mates of L. Q. Benoit, as well as those of Al Theriot and his two accomplices, C. K. and Donat Judice.

After sending the message, I went to the *New Orleans Pica-yune* archives, where I read about the robbery. There was not all that much to it. Several months later, an article covering Theriot's arrest, trial, and sentencing came out, and, finally, one last article covering Theriot's death in prison.

Continuing my search, I gathered material regarding Big Tim Strollo. As far as the media went, he was clean in regard to the heist. According to his nephew, Anthony O'Donnell, Strollo financed the casino, a financial undertaking of Herculean proportions, well into the multi-millions back in the late nineties, millions that could have come from the heist.

I Googled Jimmy Ramsey, the only former owner said to be still alive, and learned that upon his retirement from the Texas school system, he'd moved to Louisiana, where he'd leased a cabin on Ghost Bayou. According to the *Priouxville Bayou,* he'd then bought the house from Theriot a few months before the jewel heist.

Another article reported he had been too free with school money and, at the age of sixty-one, took his retirement. That would put him in his mid-seventies now. Further searching came up with two Jimmy Ramseys in New Orleans, both seventy-four.

I promptly dialed the first number under the pretext of a boyhood chum searching for an elementary pal in New Orleans. Luck was with me, for the first Ramsey professed to having lived in New Orleans for only the last six years.

The second Ramsey had lived in New Orleans all his life.

Further research on Ramsey number one told me he owned a multistory haunted house in the middle of the French Quarter and provided guided tours through it. I leaned back and studied the screen. Real estate in New Orleans wasn't cheap, not even after Hurricane Katrina. A twenty-by-forty apartment still went for up to half a million.

Made me wonder what a three-story would cost. Eight million? Or more?

There wasn't much on Theriot, so I figured on paying his former partner, Oscar Mouton, a visit at Bayou Country Motors. The last couple of members of the Prioux family were in a nursing facility. The skeptic in me wondered just how they paid for it.

Chapter Eleven

I jumped when a voice sounded directly behind me. "Still working?"

I glanced over my shoulder. "Yeah. How was your nap?"

Diane yawned and stretched her arms over her head. "Great. I feel like a new woman." She glanced at my laptop screen. "What are you working on?"

"Nothing much. Just messing around. What time do you want to go back to the hospital?" While replying, I copied all my work to the ever-present flash drive that had saved my computerized life more than once, and then closed the program. After booting off, I slipped the flash drive into my pocket.

She touched her forefinger to her pursed lips. The bright red on her nails matched her lipstick. "I don't know. Probably soon. Jack and I talked about it, and he wants me to stay here tonight. He says I'll rest better, and I probably would, knowing that you're here."

My heart flip-flopped.

She drew a deep breath and added, "But I want to be with him."

A thousand-pound weight slid off my shoulders. "Whatever you want. I've got some running around to take care of after I leave you at the hospital."

"Oh. Like what?"

I crawfished. "Nothing important."

Despite our being married for only a couple of years, she knew me well enough to know when I was hedging. "About Jack?"

"I'm not sure," I replied noncommittally.

She gave me a skeptical look. "Come on, Tony. Tell me the truth."

"You don't quit, do you?" I asked.

"No," she said sharply. "What affects him, affects me. Something is going on around here, and I want to know what it is. I deserve to know. That's what marriage is all about," she added, giving me one of those I-told-you-so looks.

I sensed the insinuation in her words. "I can't argue with you there. Yeah, it's about Jack, and this house. And about everything going on around here." I could have stopped there, but her implication that I was to blame for our divorce irritated me, so I continued. "You remember Jack said that the goons who worked him over kept asking about diamonds?"

"Yeah. So?"

"So, for your information, there are some very serious people out there who believe the diamonds are hidden somewhere on the premises." I started to tell her about the muggers running loose but decided that would be a bit of overkill.

"What?" She stared at me in disbelief.

"You heard me. One of the previous owners of this place heisted a jewelry store. The diamonds were never recovered. People of all sorts think the jewels are here. That's the reason for the prowlers."

"But are you sure?"

"Positive. That's why I want you to stay at the hospital until I come back. I don't want you out here at night by yourself. In fact, you don't need to be out here anytime by yourself until this is all settled."

"You mean, you think they might harm me?" she stammered, her eyes wide with alarm.

"Let's say that I don't want to take the chance. When you get to the hospital, you stay there. Don't leave until I let you know I'm back."

"Where are you going?"

"To see a guy about some diamonds."

During my drive out to the car dealership, I came up with

what I figured was a surefire pretext. Knowing that most people are more cooperative if they stand to gain something from their efforts, I planned to admit I was searching for the jewels for the 25 percent reward, and if I found them, I would make it worthwhile to anyone who assisted me.

Bayou Country Motors was a General Motors franchise, a ten-acre plant covered with automobiles, pickups, and a complete service and repair department.

In a way, I was surprised to see such a large dealership in such a small community, but I realized the plant not only served Priouxville, but also Baldwin, Charenton, Franklin, and Oaklawn.

I found Oscar Mouton in his spacious office on the second floor of his salesroom. Large glass panels filled one wall overlooking the sales floor below.

A short, smiling salesman with curly black hair and a down-home greeting that made you feel as if he were doing you a great favor by permitting you to purchase one of his vehicles, Mouton was the epitome of the amiable Cajun. I almost expected him to pull out a burlap-covered quart jar from under his desk and offer me a drink of moonshine. He gestured to a chair in front of his desk. His smile growing even wider, he said, "What can I do for you, Mr. Boudreaux?"

When I mentioned Al Theriot, the smile faded from his face. He stared at me a moment, his dark eyes sizing me up. "You the law?"

I gave him my little-boy-lost smile. "No. Just a friend of the guy who owns Theriot's old house, that's all." I paused. "I have a few questions about Mr. Theriot I was hoping you could help me with."

"About the robbery?"

"Yes."

He pursed his lips and shook his head. After several moments, he replied, "That be something I don't like to think about. It be long gone. Me, I want to leave it that way."

"Not even for a share of the reward for the remaining diamonds?"

I could see the wheels spinning in his head. "Reward? How much?"

"There's a 25 percent reward for the return of any or all the jewels. Could be up to a million or more."

The figure was enticing enough to elicit a touch of greed and a sheepish smirk. He shrugged. "Poor Theriot. That be sad, sad thing. Me, I couldn't believe what I hear. Even when Theriot, he admit he steal the jewels, I find it hard to believe."

"You were partners a long time, huh?"

"*Oui.* Al and me, we go to school with the nuns up to Charenton from the time the two of us, we be little *tétards,* tadpoles. That one, he be like *mon frère,* my brother." With an embarrassed grin and a slight shrug of his shoulders, he added, "Me, I thought I knew everything there was to know about him."

I leaned back in my chair. "Any idea why he pulled the job?"

He rose from his desk and crossed the room to a highboy next to one wall. Above the highboy was a large picture of his dealership taken from the air. He poured a glass of water from a crystal decanter and offered me one. I declined.

For several moments, Mouton stared at me, as if considering just how to respond. "Like I say, Al and me, we grow up together. We opened our first car lot in 1970. Five years later, we got the GM franchise." He paused to sip his water. When he finished, he held the glass up. "Us, we were on a roll. The profits, we put back into the company. By 1980, Al and me, we were living high off the hog. Me, I was satisfied. Al, he wanted more. He started investing in shaky deals." With a shrug, he shook his shoulders and returned to his desk. "Most of them blew up in his face. I tried to talk him out of them, to bring him back to his senses. No luck. That be when we started growing apart. I lent him over a hundred thousand against my better judgment. He lost that. Then he started at the casinos. For a while, he won, but then the losing started. He wanted me to buy his share of the business. I refused." His brow knit. "He accused me of trying to steal his share of the business."

I remained silent.

Several long seconds passed. The clock on the wall chimed six times.

He cleared his throat. "You ever have a good friend, *mon ami?* I mean one you loved better than a brother?"

I shook my head. "No."

His eyes grew misty. "Me, I did. Al. I couldn't stand to see that one wasting everything he'd worked so hard to earn, so I said no when he offered me his share." Ruefully, he added, "Smart me, I figured he'd have to straighten out, since there was no more money coming his way." He drew a deep breath and released it. "Well, Mr. Boudreaux, like most old men who think they know better, I was wrong. Three months later, he robbed the jewelry store. I didn't find out until later that he owed some mobster up in Alexandria almost half a million dollars."

I whistled softly. "So, he figured the heist could even him up."

Mouton opened an ornate humidor on his desk and pulled out a cigar. He offered me one, but I declined. He lit it, took a deep drag, and then blew the smoke into the air. "Crazy idea, huh?"

I remained silent a moment. "Why didn't he put up his share of the business to the mobster as collateral?"

An embarrassed smile played over his face. "Our contract. Neither of us could sell out except to each other."

With a strong hint of skepticism, I asked, "What if one died?"

"The other got it."

Nice little deal, providing you're the survivor, I told myself.

He continued, "You know, Mr. Boudreaux, I often wondered what would have happened if I'd given Al the money."

I started to reply but changed my mind.

He continued, "Me, I know what would happen. He would have lost it too. So"—he shrugged—"what was I to do?"

"Does he have any family around?"

"Al was the only child. His papa, he die when Al was a boy. His mama, she die a couple years later. After Al die, I donate his share of earnings to the Catholic Church."

I began to look at him a little differently.

"No way, me, I could keep his money."

"And he didn't give you any sort of hint as to where he hid the diamonds?"

Mouton laughed, but it was a sad laugh. "Not me, *mon ami*. Me, I be the last one. At the end, he hated me. Even when I went to the prison to see him, he don't want me there. No, me, I got no idea." He hesitated. "But there might be one. I don't know if he still be alive, but Al, he always take a shine to one Cajun boy named Lester Percher. Lester, he do odd jobs for Al. Sometimes he stay at Al's place out on the bayou."

My hopes soared. Maybe this Percher knew something of the diamonds. Maybe he was the one who'd been prowling around. "Any idea where I could find him?"

Mouton stroked his chin thoughtfully and then reached for the phone. He glanced at me. "Maybe." He punched in a couple of numbers. "Pete! This be Oscar. You remember that one they call Lester Percher? *Oui*. You know where he be?" He glanced at me. "*Oui, oui*. Okay." He replaced the receiver. "That be Pete Forest, service manager in the shop. He say Lester come from camp in Duck Lake out in the swamp, on the other side of Six Mile Lake. He forget the name of the camp. He don't know if Lester be there or not, but that be where Lester, he come from."

Chapter Twelve

There was never any question in my mind as to whether I was going to Duck Lake or not. The only question was how I was going to find it. Making your way through a swamp or through canebrakes is as confusing as maintaining a direct course through a forest of pine trees. Everything looks the same in all four directions. What few signs you might find to lead you back are usually so small or so common that they offer no help.

By the time I got back to Jack's place on the bayou, the sun had set. Back to the east, an unknown menace seemed to be lurking within the dark shadows of the deep swamp, a black hole ready to swallow any who ventured into it.

I couldn't help thinking about the flickering lights from the night before and old Rouly's dire warning of the *feu follet*. A myth, I knew, but still—there were those lights.

Turning on the living room light and the outside lights, I placed a tiny thread between the door and the jamb. There'd been enough prowlers around that I was concerned.

Then I fired up Jack's Mako and ran up the bayou to the Naquin place, grateful for the spotlight on the boat. I glanced at my watch: after seven. As soon as I hired Valsin Naquin to run me over to Duck Lake first thing the next morning, I would make a visit to the Sparkle Paradise and see what else I could find out about Harry Guzik.

The black water of the swamp teemed with life. Wherever I turned the spotlight, I picked up the bright red coals of alligator eyes like strands of Christmas lights. I shivered. They were so numerous, no one could make it twenty feet in that water. I shook my head at the plodding bureaucracy that still had alligators on the protected-species list. At any given time, I figured I was staring at enough reptiles to make boots for half the drugstore cowboys in Texas, Arizona, and New Mexico.

As I approached the Naquins', I swept my light across the dock, spotting not only their three boats, but an extra one, an aluminum eighteen-footer with a hundred-horsepower Yamaha engine.

I had no sooner bumped the dock than three floodlights came on, lighting the area like daytime, leaving me staring at a three-foot alligator on the pier.

For a moment, we stared at each other. Before I could jump back, the little teenager flipped around in his tracks and squirted over the far side of the dock. At the far end of the pier, two or three water snakes slithered into the water.

A voice from above called out, "Hey!"

I peered up but could make out only the silhouette of a man. I shaded my eyes against the floodlights and called back, "Hey!"

"What you need?"

"I want to hire Valsin to take me over to some camp in Duck Lake in the morning. On the other side of Six Mile Lake."

"Where to? Cocodrie Slough?"

Cocodrie Slough! I shivered. *Alligator Slough.* That sure didn't sound inviting. With a shrug, I replied, "If that's the only one on Duck Lake."

The head bobbed. "Come on up, you. We talk in the house."

By now, the lights had cleared the myriad reptiles from the pier.

Clerville was waiting for me at the top of the stairs. He greeted me like a long-lost relative and ushered me into the house. I hesitated, spotting old Rouly at the table, a lopsided smile on his weathered face.

"Hey, Boudreaux."

"Mr. Rouly."

Naquin gestured to a chair at the kitchen table that was covered by a red-and-white-checkered oilcloth. "Sit." He glanced at his wife. "Coffee, Zozette." He slid in at the table. "Me and Rouly here was just visiting and enjoying our coffee."

By now the three Naquin sons, wearing shorts and sagging T-shirts, had filed through the door and stood staring at me curiously.

"Hi."

They muttered a greeting.

Zozette set a small demitasse of thick black coffee before me with a small spoon and a bowl of sugar. Clerville smiled up at his wife and laid a scarred hand on hers. *"Vous remercier, mon doux." Thank you, my sweet.*

I sipped the coffee and smacked my lips. "Just like I get back home in Church Point." I turned to Clerville. "I'm not interrupting anything, am I? I can come back."

Rouly spoke up. "No, no. Me, I come drink coffee and try to out-lie old Clerville here. Been trying for thirty years now and still ain't done it."

We all laughed.

"So," Clerville said. "What's this about Valsin?"

I glanced at the three men standing in the doorway. "Well, Mr. Naquin, I—"

He shook his head. "Me, I be Clerville to my friends."

A warm feeling washed over me. "All right, Clerville. I need to find a man over at Cocodrie Slough. I don't know how to get there. I figured Valsin or one of your boys could show me the way."

The small man frowned. "Who this one you be looking for?"

It is never a good idea to reveal all you know about a case, but I had no choice if I wanted help. "Name's Percher, Lester Percher. He—"

Rouly interrupted. "He be the one what be friends with old Theriot what robbed the jewels in New Orleans." He looked at Clerville. "You remember that?"

"Oui, I remember."

The two remained silent, staring at each other. Then, as one, they looked back at me.

I explained. "That's right. I want to see what he knows about the jewels. I talked to the sheriff, and he told me about the murders in the last few weeks."

Rouly nodded. "*Oui*. You talk about Charley Primeaux and Dudley Vitale."

"Yeah."

Clerville grunted. "At least old Benoit, he got somebody to play *bourré* with now."

Bourré was Cajun poker, cutthroat to the end. Everyone played it, but as the old saying goes, to play *bourré,* you had to learn the hard way, by standing in your crib. "What do you mean?"

Rouly answered for him. "Vitale and Primeaux, they was Benoit's card-playing partners. Why, those three, they played ever' Friday night since I can remember. The loup-garou, he get them before Benoit, he come back from prison. He mighty sad when he hear about them."

"Oh. Well, like I told the sheriff, maybe this last one, Benoit, found out about the jewels in prison, and someone either shut him up or killed him when they tried to find out what he knew."

Rouly spoke up. "No. Like me, I tell you, that be the loup-garou what kill old Benoit, just like it kill Vitale and Primeaux."

"No disrespect intended, Mr. Rouly, but whoever killed those three was human, just like us."

His eyes blazing, he stared at me for several moments, then pushed back from the chair. "Me, I know what I know. It be the loup-garou." He pointed a bent and gnarled finger at me. "You see. You see. That one, he be out in the swamp right now, watching, blinking them red eyes of his up and down, up and down."

Without another word, he turned on his heel and left.

I smiled apologetically at Clerville. "Sorry. I didn't mean to upset him."

The older man sighed in resignation. "Old Rouly, he got a temper, that one. Don't you worry none about it. Anyways, talking about them two, Charley and Dudley, they not only played cards with Benoit, but they be town drunks along with him too."

I filed that little piece of information away in the back of my head. Three drinking buddies? Three *bourré* partners? Few secrets there. Chances were, I told myself, Benoit told those two what he knew. "Tell me something, Clerville. Would you happen to know if Primeaux or Vitale ever paid Benoit a visit while he was in prison?"

A frown creased the wiry Chitimacha Indian's face. He looked at his sons.

Valsin grunted. "Primeaux, he go up to the prison by himself just before Christmas one year, maybe more. Me, I ain't certain." He pursed his lips. "Why you ask?"

"Just curious," I replied. "Just curious." What I didn't tell him was that he had just handed me a dandy motive for the murder of Charley Primeaux and Dudley Vitale.

Clerville spoke to Valsin. "You hear what Tony say about Duck Lake? He need someone to take him to Cocodrie Slough. Your brothers got to run crab lines tomorrow morning before dragging for shrimp."

Hastily, I put in, "Naturally, I'll pay you for taking me, whatever the going rate is."

He grinned, his white teeth a brilliant contrast to his dark-complexioned skin. He waved as if to say forget it. "I show you the way. No problem."

"No," I refused. "Fifty bucks. That's what I'll pay you. It shouldn't take more than a few hours, huh?"

Valsin glanced at his father, who nodded almost imperceptibly. With a slight shrug, the tall, lean Chitimacha said, "*Oui*. Fifty dollars. But we go tonight."

"Tonight?" I stared at him in disbelief. "You mean in the dark? Through the swamp? Across the lake?"

His younger brother, August, explained, "It not be dark. There be stars."

"*Oui*. And the moon, it comes up in a couple hours," added the middle brother, Dolzin.

"Besides," Valsin put in, "me, I got work to do tomorrow."

I looked back at Clerville. He indicated his older son. "That one, he find his way though the swamp with his eyes closed."

I stared out the window in the direction of the swamps. Those sprawling watery forests were forbidding enough during daylight. But at night—all I could think of were those eerie flickering lights, even though I knew they were probably just fireflies or even nighttime fishermen. Besides, I had planned on paying a visit to the Sparkle Paradise.

Valsin slapped me on the shoulder. "Let's go, Tony. It be seven thirty. We get there by nine."

Dolzin spoke up. "If it be all right with you, Mr. Boudreaux, I'd just as soon go along for the ride." He stuck his tongue out at his younger brother, August. "This one, he not much good at Wii Golf. Besides, I know some of the boys at Cocodrie."

August punched Dolzin on the shoulder playfully. "Look who be talking. Me, I win the last three games. You best stay here and practice. I'll go. I know the same old boys you know. I say hi for you."

Valsin settled the argument. "We all know them. Come on if you want."

Five minutes later, we pushed away from the dock, with Valsin behind the wheel of the Mako, me beside him on the bench, and the two brothers in front. Dolzin cradled a pint jar of potent moonshine between his legs. We ran about a hundred yards upriver, where Valsin took a starboard turn into the forbidding swamp. Starlight filtered down through the canopy of cypress needles, laying out undulating strips of bluish light on the dark water.

Even though we were moving at only a moderate speed, I clutched the console for dear life. Peering into the almost absolute darkness, I managed to croak out, "I've got a spotlight if you want to use it."

"Don't you now be worrying, Tony. The light, it blinds me. I come this way so much, I know it by heart. Just relax, you. Look at Dolzin up there. Me, I wouldn't be surprised if he was sleeping like a baby."

I didn't bother to look, for I was too busy clinging to the console. Every moment, I expected the jarring impact and screeching rip as we ran upon an immovable cypress knee.

His eyes on the invisible trail ahead of him, Valsin said, "This Percher. Me, I know the man. He shrimps Six Mile Lake and the bayous."

I looked up. "His own boat?"

"Oui."

I didn't think much more of his remark, figuring he was speaking of one of the smaller eighteen- to twenty-foot boats most of the small shrimpers used.

Other than the purr of the engine and the bow slicing through the dark waters, the only sounds were the cry of loons, the harrumphing of bullfrogs, and the bellowing of alligators. The first two I didn't concern myself with, but the last one worried me.

Even the two younger brothers remained silent.

After thirty minutes of praying, sweating, and cursing, I sighed with relief when we emerged from the swamp onto the black expanse of Six Mile Lake. To the east, a few dim lights glittered in the darkness, a welcome beacon.

Dolzin broke out the jar to celebrate.

Chapter Thirteen

We skirted the shores of Six Mile Lake and found the entrance to Duck Lake. The cold, dim lights of Cocodrie Slough winked on the far shore. It was not yet nine.

Valsin chuckled, his white teeth standing out in the starlight. Back to the east, the waning moon rose over a forest of ten-foot-tall cane. "We make good time, Tony. We be at Cocodrie Slough in fifteen minutes."

Although I hadn't invited August and Dolzin to make the trip with us, when I spotted the small village squatting on a rickety sprawl of ancient docks and piers a few feet above the water of Duck Lake, I was glad they'd come along.

I knew from experience the inhabitants of these isolated villages were a breed apart from even those who lived on the fringes of civilization back across the lake.

As we drew closer, the hum of generators rolled across the water. At one end of the village, where the bayou deepened, a dozen boats of all sizes lay at anchor. Tiny bateaux, or johnboats, were tied at the base of piers supporting the structures of the village. Rickety ladders descended from the wooden walkways down to the boats.

One of the clapboard structures had a string of Christmas lights dangling from the front eaves. Rollicking accordion and fiddle music mixed with raucous laughter rolled out the open windows and spilled across the bayou. The local honky-tonk.

Valsin pulled up a few houses away from the saloon. "Me, I think we find Percher in there," he announced, taking a drink before clambering up the ladder to the walkway overhead.

Dolzin offered me the jar, but I declined. My stomach was a pit of butterflies. I didn't want any false courage getting me into a jam I couldn't get out of. I hurried up the ladder.

While he and I waited for his brothers to climb up, he pointed out a ninety-foot freezer shrimp boat moored at a dock farther up the bayou. "That be Percher's boat," he said.

I whistled softly. That was a two-hundred-thousand-dollar boat. "Not bad," I replied.

In a furtive tone, Valsin said, "There be talk at the time how that one, he come up with the money. He was always the *clo-chard*, the bum what never had nothing but what he begged." He paused and then continued. "One day, he the *clochard;* he got nothing. The next—" He held the palm of his hand out toward the boat and, his voice heavy with sarcasm, added, "Then, *alors, comme un miracle.* There it be, the shrimp boat."

I surveyed the boat, my suspicions growing by the second. That was big money for a dirt-poor Cajun boy. How had he come up with it? I had an idea, and it wasn't the Louisiana lottery. "He must make big hauls in that. Where does he sell them?"

"Down to Morgan City and around," Valsin replied.

Dolzin's clambering up the ladder pulled me back to the present. I handed Valsin several twenties. "If Percher's in there, buy drinks for the house. I'll get him aside."

The red and green Christmas lights glittered on the amused gleam in his eyes. "Me, I think I like you, Boudreaux."

There were a dozen or so fishermen and a handful of women inside. Everything grew silent when we entered, even the fiddle and accordion. We stopped and looked around, and then Valsin raised his hand and called out, "Bernard! Moise! How you old boys be?"

As soon as the bar patrons recognized the Naquin brothers, the celebration began again. I sort of slipped up to the bar with the brothers, trying to lose myself in their midst.

Everyone had gathered around us, joking, shaking hands, offering drinks. Since I was with the brothers, the rough fisher-men took me as one of their own.

After a few minutes at the bar sipping cold Abita Bock beer

and eyeing the crowd, Valsin moved to my side. "Your man, he be at the end of the bar. The one with the red shirt. The *peeshwank,* the runt."

Wearing overalls over a grimy T-shirt, Lester leaned against the bar with another fisherman. Most Cajuns who topped five feet ten or so were considered tall, but Valsin was right in his assessment of Lester Percher. He was a *peeshwank,* a runt at about five-six. He had the typical curly black hair of the true Cajun, and his swarthy complexion reflected years of sunlight and weather.

I had decided to be honest with him, or as honest as I could be. Lester, I figured, would jump at the chance for a reward, unless he had a stash of diamonds put away. Before I pushed away from the bar, August, who stood on my other side, whispered, "Don't look now, *mon ami,* but there be a *jeune dame* that be sweet-eyeing you." He glanced across the smoke-filled room.

I have yet to see a dusky-complexioned young woman from the backwaters of the Louisiana swamps who doesn't project a haunting beauty that lingers in the mind like fresh dewdrops on the dark green leaves of lemon trees.

When she saw me, she smiled, her brilliant white teeth a sharp contrast to her tawny skin. I started to smile back, but when I saw the two men with her glare, I looked away hastily.

Grabbing my bottle of beer, I moved down the bar to Lester.

The two men looked around when I stopped by their side.

I offered my hand. I almost had to shout to be heard above the riotous clamor in the bar. "Name's Boudreaux. I came over here with the Naquin brothers."

Both men shot suspicious glances over my shoulder, but when they spotted the brothers, they relaxed. Lester took my hand and introduced himself. "And this ugly *aucun compte,* he be Juju Broussard."

I knew the expression *aucun compte* to mean "no-account," an affable tag that friends placed on each other. I took Juju's hand. "Happy to meet you. Buy you a beer?"

Lester chugged the rest of his brew. "Me, I never turn down free beer."

Juju patted his belly. "Me neither."

After paying for the drinks, I turned back to Lester. "I came here to talk business."

The short Cajun frowned at me and then looked around at Juju, who simply shrugged. "Shrimping? Me, I got plenty business doing that," Lester replied.

Juju agreed. "Us, we don't need no more right now. We just come back from three weeks out in the Gulf."

I cursed under my breath. Juju had just blown my theory of Lester prowling around Jack's house. I shook my head. "No—no shrimping, Lester. I want to talk to you about Al Theriot."

His eyes grew wide in shock, then narrowed warily.

Continuing, I assured him, "I'm no cop. Not the law." I looked around the raucous honky-tonk and joked, "No cop in his right mind would come over here."

"That be true," Juju said with a leer.

I almost shouted, "I'm just an average Cajun boy who wants to make some money, and I'm offering you a cut."

Lester studied me, trying to decide if I were lying or not. Finally, he turned to Juju and rattled off Cajun French so softly, I couldn't make out his words. The only one I picked up on was *seul,* which meant "alone." He pointed the beer bottle at an empty table. "Over there."

His eyes remained wary as we slid in at the table. He leaned back in his chair. "All right, Boudreaux, what you got in mind?"

"You were close friends with Theriot." I made it a statement, not a question.

He shrugged.

"I mean, you spent time with him, worked for him at the car lot, stayed at his house sometimes. That sort of thing, right?"

Another shrug. "Some," he replied indifferently.

Resting my elbows on the table, I leaned forward so he could hear me better. "All right. Now here's the deal. Theriot heisted a jewel store in New Orleans. He hid the loot before the cops got him. He and his partners, the Judice brothers, were wasted in prison."

"Yeah. Me, I know that."

"A friend of mine bought the house Theriot owned on Ghost Bayou. Prowlers have been searching for the diamonds. That's when I learned that there's a reward for them. Maybe two million, more or less, and I'm willing to give you a sizable cut if you can point me in their direction."

His eyes grew wide, then narrowed furtively. "You think, me, I know where the diamonds be?" There was a hint of amusement in his eyes and a faint smile on his face, as if he were keeping a secret from me.

"No. But I figured if we talked some, I might get a hint where to start looking. Of course, somebody knows something, because if you remember reading about it, some of the loot turned up a few years ago. Story I heard was they were found in a pawnshop up in Alexandria."

His smile grew wider. With exaggerated innocence, he replied, "You know, I think me, I hear that too. You know?"

I had the feeling right then he was playing with me, jacking me around. "Oh?"

"You see the big shrimp boat out in the bayou when you come in?"

"Yeah. Valsin said it belongs to you."

"That be right."

I remembered Valsin's remark about people wondering among themselves where Lester came up with the money. "Nice boat."

His eyes glittered with satisfaction. "You think me, I'd be here if I knew where old Theriot hid them other diamonds?" He shook his head. "But you right about some of the haul turning up in Alexandria. How you think I got that shrimp boat out there?"

Chapter Fourteen

I surprised him when I replied, "I figured as much when I saw the boat."

"What's that?"

"When I heard about the time you spent with Theriot, I had a hunch you might know something. What I can't figure is why you weren't in on the heist with him instead of the Judice brothers."

His brow knit in anger for a moment. "That be Theriot's mistake. Me, the law would never find, not back out here in the swamps. C. K., he knew what he was doing, but Donat, that one, he started blubbering when the law hauled him in." He turned up his beer and drained it. "Old Donat, he never good up here," he said, tapping the side of his head with the top of his empty beer bottle.

"Where'd you find the diamonds?"

"Somewhere."

I leaned back in the chair. "Keeping it a secret, huh? Can't say I blame you, except, with all the new technology out there today, laundering them will be a whole lot harder than a few years ago."

He grew serious. "Me, I know that. That be why I don't look for them. Oh, they be out there, but there be too many who want to put their sticky fingers on them to suit me." He paused and added, "I don't figure I would live a week if I tried to move them diamonds." He shrugged. "That's why I don't worry none about them, even if I knew where they be." He set the empty bottle on the table. "Which I don't."

I studied him for a moment. For some reason, I believed him. I held up two fingers to the waitress behind the bar. She nodded, and I looked back around, straight into the eyes of the little

Cajun girl who had smiled at me earlier. She was leaning over, her chest brushing my shoulder. "Buy me a beer, *cher?*"

The waitress plopped Abita Bock beers down in front of us on the table. I shot a hasty glance at the two locals with whom she had been drinking. "Maybe later," I said, turning back to Lester.

Eyes blazing, she jerked upright and then stormed back to her table.

If I'd paid attention, I would have seen her jabbering to the locals with whom she'd been drinking and jabbing her finger at me. I would have known trouble was just around the corner, ready to tap me on the shoulder with a beer bottle in its hand.

I took a sip of my beer and then cleared my throat. "Did you find the diamonds yourself?"

He pressed his lips together and shook his head. "Hard to remember," he finally said.

In my line of work, I had become a master in recognizing delay, or stalling, or hedging. That's what crafty Lester Percher was doing. "Tell you what. I'll guarantee you 10 percent of what I find. That could be as little as two hundred thousand, and—who knows?—as much as eight hundred big ones." I was just pulling figures out of the air.

His face remained impassive. "How do I know I can trust you?"

"Don't worry. There ain't no way, my friend, that I would try to peddle the diamonds. They're registered, and I don't care nothing about fifteen or twenty years at Angola or Winn, even for eight million bucks. I'll return the diamonds and settle for two million or whatever." I paused and then added, "You might as well take the gamble. As it stands now, you got no chance at them. Me, I got one. If it doesn't pan out, then you've always got your shrimp boat, right?"

"*Oui,* me, I always got the shrimp boat." He took a long drink of beer. He drew the back of his hand across his lips. "All right, I tell you what you ask, Boudreaux. You see, Theriot sell the house to a Texas school superintendent or something like that."

A shrimper entered the bar. An anomaly among Cajuns, he stood well over six feet and topped two-fifty at a minimum. He wore a thick black Santa Claus type beard and even blacker hair down to his shoulders. He glanced around. His eyes touched on me and continued until he found the two crabbers seated at the table with the angry Cajun woman.

I looked back at Percher. "You mean Ramsey. Jimmy Ramsey."

"*Oui, oui.* I don't know much about Ramsey, but he had a cousin, K. D. Dople, what lived in Priouxville. Had for years. K. D., he come to me. He'd learned where some of the diamonds was hid, but he got sent to prison. When he got out, he come over here. Said it would take two of us to pull it off."

My pulse quickened. Now I was on the track of the diamonds. "How did he find out about them?"

"He never say. When me, I ask, he just laugh and say it none of my business. He say I wouldn't believe it if he told me the truth. But he say over and over we got no time to waste."

"Why?"

Lester reached under the bib of his overalls and fished a battered pack of Lucky Strikes from the pocket of his T-shirt. He lit one, inhaled, and squinted as the smoke drifted slowly to the ceiling. "Don't know. Me, I not be sure. I got the feeling he heard something from the superintendent cousin of his."

"Ramsey?"

He paused. "*Oui.* But me, I ain't sure. Maybe from that Guzik what got himself killed last year, or maybe Theriot told him."

"You mean Dople worked for all three?"

Lester chugged a couple of swallows of beer. "*Oui.*"

"This Dople guy, where can I find him? He still live in Priouxville?"

"*Mais non.* He be dead now."

I grimaced. So much for being on the trail of the diamonds.

He continued. "*Oui,* he be shot dead in a ditch over to Vernon Parish. The law say it be a gang killing. K. D., that one, he gamble like *un homme fou.*"

I grinned. "A crazy man, huh?"

Percher grunted. "*Oui.*"

"You don't think it had anything to do with the diamonds?"

He pursed his lips, his bearded cheeks sunken in his angular face. "I think maybe at first that be the reason, but then talk come in about the gambling."

"Why did he come to you?"

Percher shrugged. "For years, I work for Theriot at his car lot. Me, I know every inch of the place. Dople, he know I can get him inside without nobody knowing nothing." He gave me a sly look. "And me, I did."

"So, where were the diamonds?"

He chugged down three or four gulps of Abita, drew his hand across his lips, and leaned forward. "When they robbed the jewelry store, Theriot and Mouton, they was building four more service bays at the dealership. Just after the bricklayers lay the first few rows of cinder blocks, Theriot, he go out at night and place the metal box with the diamonds in a corner block on the first layer. He puts cement on top, and next morning, the bricklayers keep right on laying them concrete blocks."

I stared at him in disbelief, and then the wisdom of such a hiding spot dawned on me. From the corner of my eye, I saw Dolzin coming toward me. I turned back to Percher, but before I could ask the next question, a rough hand grabbed my shoulder and jerked me around.

I almost fell out of my chair. When I looked up, I was staring into the drunken faces of two enraged Cajun crabbers. Standing behind them was the leering face of the shrimper who had just come in, and next to him was the sweet little Cajun flower whose lovely little face had morphed into the grotesque countenance of the witch hags in *Macbeth*.

I wish I could say I thought fast, but I didn't. In the next second, one of the crabbers stuck his unshaven face in mine. Despite the fact I'd had a couple beers, I could smell the stench of a dozen on his breath.

Through half a dozen missing teeth, he bellowed, "What for you come out here and insult one of our ladies?"

"That be right!" shouted his partner, who was standing at his side. "We don't need no *étrangers* coming in here and helping make fools of us."

The young woman looked up at him angrily. "What do you mean by that?"

Before I could reply, Lester, exhibiting the hot temper of every *peeshwank* I've ever known, stood up and put his hand in the first one's chest. "Easy there, Hulin. Easy. This one, he don't offend Ruth." In a half-joking, half-serious tone, he said, "Me, I don't know of nobody what can offend that girl, you know?"

Angrily, Hulin slapped Lester's hand away. "You stay out of this, Percher. This be between me and this one." The incensed crabber turned back to me. By now, I had pushed to my feet.

That's all Lester needed. Once again, before I could reply, Lester stepped in and swung his full bottle of beer at Hulin's head.

The wiry Cajun threw his arm up, taking the major impact on his forearm, but the bottle slid off and whopped him on the forehead, cutting a slice in his skin and sending him stumbling backward. With a wild shout, he threw out his arms for balance, knocking both his partner and Ruth back into the oversized shrimper.

Someone grabbed my arm and spun me around. By then his partner, I'd had enough of the manhandling. I cocked my right fist but then saw it was Dolzin.

"Quick. Out of here."

I didn't argue. Half a dozen shrimpers and fisherman were heading in our direction.

August and Valsin stepped in to stop them. In the blink of an eye, the fight erupted.

Chairs whizzed through the air. Bottles and cans smashed and clattered against the clapboard walls. Men cursed and grunted. Even a couple of tables took to the air. All through the melee, the fiddler and accordion player never missed a beat.

Valsin shouted at Dolzin, "Get Boudreaux out of here!"

Dolzin dragged me after him, but before we made it to the door, two crabbers jumped in front of us. "You boys ain't going nowhere," one of them said. The other one leered at us.

Dolzin said, "Look, Paul. Us, we didn't come over here for trouble. My friend here, he just needed to talk to Lester a few minutes. He sure didn't mean no offense to Ruth there."

We all glanced back at the young woman who was trying, without success, to gracefully extricate herself from the tangle of chairs into which she had fallen.

With a lecherous gleam in his eye, Paul remarked, "That Ruth, she be something else, don't that be right, Dolzin?"

The young man's response was a sharp kick in the groin. When Paul jerked forward to grab at the pain, Dolzin caught him with a right uppercut, sending the crabber to the floor unconscious.

Just as Dolzin hit Paul, I charged Hulin's partner, smashing my shoulder into his oversized belly and slamming him through the door and out onto the walkway. I backed away a step and threw a straight right, catching the unprepared crabber on the point of the chin and knocking him over the rail into the neck-deep water below.

A knotty fist caught me on the back of my head, sending me stumbling to the walkway. I rolled over just as a rubber boot stomped into the weathered wood beside my head. Instinctively, I rolled up into a sitting position and threw a left hook, catching my assailant in the same spot Dolzin had struck his.

With a wild scream, my assailant doubled over. I leaped to my feet and, grabbing him by the collar and the seat of his overalls, ran him off the walkway into the water.

A weight hit me on the back, sending me stumbling forward. I threw up my arms for protection and tried to turn and face the blows raining down on me. My assailant was a young man in his late teens or early twenties, the prime of his life, with muscles he'd never used.

He caught me with a roundhouse right that exploded stars in my head and made my ears ring. In the eerie shadows cast by the red and green Christmas lights, blows had a way of sneaking up on you.

I caught one of his wild lefts on my right forearm, then jabbed his sneering face a couple of times, knocking him back a step. Stepping forward, I threw a straight right that smashed his nose over his beardless face. He staggered back, clutching his hands to his face. When he pulled them away and saw the amount of blood on them, his eyes grew wild, and he charged me, swinging wildly.

He was stronger than me, younger than me, meaner than me. All I had going for me was fear and experience. At the last minute, I sidestepped and caught him in the side of his head with a sizzling left that sent him face-first to the wooden walk. "Don't get up, kid. Please don't get up."

My head exploded, and I fell back against the railing, fumbling at the chair someone had thrown at me.

"Boudreaux!" I threw up my fists and looked around. Valsin was waving for me to follow. He sprinted down the wooden walkway. Dolzin appeared at my side. We raced for the boat.

Four more shrimpers poured from the honky-tonk, chasing us.

Valsin had already pulled the Mako away from the pier. Dolzin and I did the only thing left to do. We leaped into the water and swam to the boat.

Back up on the walkway, several drunken shrimpers called out, "Hey there, Valsin. That be fun. You old boys come back, you hear?"

August shouted back at them, telling them good-naturedly where they could go. He turned to face us, a nice little mouse under his right eye.

Dolzin, sporting a small cut over his left eye, exclaimed, "I tell you, *mes amis,* that be one good fight."

Valsin looked over his shoulder. "You got that right, Dolzin. Now, where be that jug? This calls for a drink."

All I could do was shake my head in wonder.

Chapter Fifteen

By the time we reached the cypress swamp, I was feeling no pain. Cajun moonshine, the good stuff, was not just alcohol; it was a smooth elixir that would drive any connoisseur of wine or whiskey to the point of envy. My Grand-père Moise had had a still in his barn that Grand-mère Ola was always fussing about. He was an artist when it came to the distillation of good shine, and I swear, the Naquin shine was every bit as smooth and potent as Grand-père's.

We relived the fight, passing the jar from one to the other with practiced regularity. Valsin took a long drink, then drew the back of his hand across his swollen lips. "What do you suppose old T-Ball was doing over there?"

August shrugged. "Who knows?"

I frowned. "T-Ball?"

August snorted. "That be the big ox what come in just before the fight start. The one with the big black beard. He from Charenton. I can't figure what he was doing over there."

"Yeah, me, at first I wonder that too," Dolzin replied. "I figure he too busy tending his horses."

"He got family over there," Valsin replied.

Dolzin shrugged. "Maybe so, but I heard him ask Pete where Boudreaux was. Pete told him, and he looked at Boudreaux here real angry like. I was going to tell you about it when the fight started."

"Me?"

The younger man shrugged. "I couldn't hear what they was saying, but he was looking for you."

Valsin looked around from the wheel and snorted. "Tony be a stranger, that why."

Dolzin shook his head. "Maybe so, but it don't sound like that to me. He asked Pete to point out Boudreaux."

We rode in silence for a few minutes, the purring of the engine and the hissing of the bow cutting through the dark water the only sounds in the night.

I looked around at August. "You said this T-Ball has horses?"

"*Oui*. Quarter horses. He races them at the track," Dolzin answered.

"At the Golden Crystal?"

"*Oui*."

Valsin called over his shoulder, "Him and the sheriff, they still be *copains?*"

I looked at Dolzin. "*Copains?*"

"You know, *buddies*. The sheriff, he like to bet on the horses. T-Ball, he got some he race from time to time."

August took a deep swallow of moonshine. "*Oui,* and there be some what say Thertule, he owe a bunch of money to the wrong ones too."

Valsin snorted. "You, you don't know nothing. The sheriff, he don't owe nobody nothing. Next thing you going to tell me is that the sheriff, he be the loup-garou old Rouly claims done killed Benoit and the others."

August grew somber and quickly made the sign of the cross. "Don't joke about nothing like that. Me, I done see the sign about Benoit. It be the loup-garou."

About that time, we entered the swamp, and the moonlight filtering through the canopy of cypress needles cast eerie shadows over the youngest Naquin's face.

The alcohol had numbed my bruises, warmed my belly, and dulled my thoughts. After a few moments, his words soaked in. I looked around at August. "What do you mean, you saw the sign?"

Dolzin rolled his eyes. "Please, dear Virgin Mother, not again. This be the hundredth time he tell us."

August shoved him on the shoulder. "You shut up." He looked

around. "Me, I was going to town when Rouly, he stopped me. He was standing by the side of the road. In the ditch, there was Benoit, and all around him was tracks of the loup-garou."

"What kind of tracks?"

He shrugged. With his thumb and forefinger, he made a half circle a few inches in diameter. "Big round tracks, like this. Tracks of the horse."

The same thing old Rouly had said. Next time the jar came my way, I passed it up. I had to get the boat back down the bayou, and the last thing I wanted to do was run upon a cypress knee and fight off alligators the rest of the night.

By eleven o'clock, I was home. I noticed the thread was still between the door and the jamb. Nevertheless, I checked the house for snakes, after which I took a hot shower and whipped up a sandwich to put something in my stomach. During the hour or so since my last drink, I had metabolized some of the alcohol, and now my stomach was growling. I carried the sandwich and a glass of milk into the living room.

Sitting next to the window, I looked out over the moon-splashed bayou and swamp, listening to the night sounds. The scene brought back memories of my youth, of the mysterious and haunting bayous.

To my relief, I saw no flickering lights in the uninviting shadows of the swamp.

I had planned to drive out to the Sparkle Paradise the next morning and see what I could learn about Guzik, but I decided instead to pay Jimmy Ramsey a visit over in New Orleans. See what he could tell me about K. D. Dople.

But first, I had to visit Jack in the hospital and make some arrangements for Diane.

I padded toward the bedroom. The blinking red light on the telephone indicated voice mail. I picked up the receiver and punched in the numbers Diane had given me.

The message was from Sheriff Lacoutrue. "Boudreaux, here be the information you asked for. During Benoit's time in prison, he had four cell mates. One was Billy Arsenault from Alexandria;

Donald Carson from New Orleans; Paul Foret from Monroe; and John Boneau from Branch."

Disappointed, I jotted down the names. I was hoping Benoit had spent time with one of the Judices or even Theriot. Then I reminded myself that the latter had been wasted long before Benoit became a guest of the state.

I booted up my laptop, but to my disappointment, Eddie had not responded to my e-mail. I couldn't blame him. Less than forty-eight hours had passed, although so much had happened that it seemed like four hundred and eighty hours.

I climbed between clean, fresh sheets. All I remember was my face touching the pillow.

On the way to the hospital the next morning, I tried to sort my thoughts and put together a logical plan, but all I had were half a dozen ideas, none of which seemed to connect to one another.

I still didn't have any notion who had worked Jack over. I was well aware of the mentality of mob soldiers. Unless they have a death wish, they'll never lie to their bosses. That's why I couldn't believe Carl and Patsy were responsible for Jack.

If not those two, who?

Parking in front of the hospital, I leaned on the steering wheel and stared blankly through the windshield. I could eliminate Lester. He'd been fishing out in the Gulf for three weeks. Then I thought about T-Ball. From the way the Naquins talked, he seldom found his way to Cocodrie Slough.

And I reminded myself, the fight had started within minutes after he arrived. Could he have some connection with Theriot or the diamonds? I leaned back and closed my eyes. I had never felt so confused in all my life. With a drawn out sigh, I climbed from the Chevy pickup and headed up the sidewalk into the hospital.

Diane was lying in the La-Z-Boy recliner, and Jack was sitting up in bed, a thick chocolate milkshake on the table beside him. His face brightened when I entered. "Hey, Tony," he mumbled between clenched teeth, the old animation back in his voice and eyes.

"Hey, Jack. You're looking good."

He winked at Diane. "I feel good." He shot a dark glance at the door. "I'm ready to get out of here, but the doc wants me to stay another day or so."

Diane rocked forward. "You know it's for your own good, sweetheart. He just wants to make sure your brains are not scrambled." She winked at me.

"Yeah," I replied. "You don't have too many in there anyway."

He muttered an amiable curse. The smile faded from his face. "What's going on?"

"Absolutely nothing, buddy. I'm not any closer to learning who worked you over than I was three days ago."

He grew serious. "What about the diamonds?"

I glanced at Diane. She smiled sheepishly. "I told him what you said about the diamonds and about me being out at the house by myself."

"You should have told me," he said.

Chuckling, I made a sweeping gesture at the bed. "And what could you have done all laid up here like one of those Egyptian mummies?"

"I know, but—"

"Look, Jack. There was nothing you could have done. There still isn't. You've just got to heal up so we can get you out of here. Then you can defend your wife to the death," I added with a touch of dramatic flair.

He sighed and leaned back against his pillow. "Yeah, you're right. Still, I feel helpless."

I eyed his cast and wired jaw. With a touch of wry sarcasm, I replied, "Well, meaning no offense, old buddy, but the way it looks to me, *helpless* just about sums up your situation."

He snorted.

I nodded at his arm. "You can't hit anybody, and you sure can't bite them. So, yeah. *Helpless* is as good a description as any."

He laughed. "I suppose so."

"Tell you what you two ought to do when you get out of here. Sell the place and get back to Austin."

Jack snorted. "No. No way. This is something I've wanted for the last couple of years."

I started to argue with him, but at that moment, a young nurse in tan scrubs entered briskly and proceeded to take Jack's vital signs. While she tended to him, I turned to Diane. "How are you this morning?"

She smiled wanly. "Fine." She laid her hand on the La-Z-Boy armrest. "This isn't the best mattress in the world. I'll be glad to get into my own bed."

I grimaced.

Before I could speak, she continued. "Something wrong?"

"No, not really. I planned to run over to New Orleans today."

She paused, realizing just how such a trip implicated her. "And you don't want me staying by myself?"

"Yeah."

She patted the armrest once again. "I'm not eager for another night in this chair. I'll go with you. I can doze on the way."

I stiffened. "My pickup's twice as uncomfortable as that chair."

"We can take the Cadillac. I'll sleep in the back." She pushed to her feet. "Don't worry. I'll be fine. We can stop at the house and pick up a couple of pillows and a blanket."

Blanket? Pillows? I tried to find some logical explanation why she shouldn't accompany me, one that would not offend her or Jack.

"And I promise not to get in your way, all right?"

"Get in whose way?" Jack asked.

Diane turned to Jack. "Tony's going to New Orleans. Like I told you, he doesn't want me to stay at the house by myself, so I'm going to ride over there with him, if you don't mind. Mr. Jay's at the vet's, so he'll be okay. Will you be all right by yourself?"

He looked up at me. "What's in New Orleans?"

"A previous owner of your house. Jimmy Ramsey. Used to be a school superintendent over in Texas." I didn't go into detail about his possible involvement with Al Theriot or his cousin or Lester Percher. "He might know something that could help us."

Jack looked skeptical. "Like what?"

"Who knows?" I shrugged. "That's how these things are.

You talk to enough people, and if you're lucky, you stumble onto something that will help."

"Yeah. I understand. You go on, babe. I'm fine here. In fact, get a gourmet dinner and spend the night at one of those fancy French Quarter hotels. Separate rooms, of course." He winked at me. "I'll be just fine here." He reached for her hand. "Besides, you need a break, sweetheart. I know it gets awfully tiring here for you."

The two gushy lovers outvoted me.

Outside, I grabbed my sports bag with a change of clothes and toiletries from the pickup and tossed them into the trunk of the Cadillac, an XLR convertible with the 4.6L V8 engine and five-speed automatic transmission. I locked the pickup and left the keys with Jack.

As we climbed into the car, sheriff Thertule Lacoutrue drove past in his cruiser. He looked at me, and I waved.

We stopped by the house so Diane could change from her dress into comfortable slacks and a baggy tunic and sandals. Quickly, she assembled a couple more changes of clothes, grabbed her makeup bag, and gave it all to me to haul out to the car. She followed with pillows, a blanket, and an ice chest with a bottle of Merlot and foam cups.

"We can stop in Lafayette and grab a hamburger," she said.

By eleven o'clock, we were on I-10 out of Lafayette heading for New Orleans, with hamburger, fries, and Merlot in foam cups.

Next stop, the City That Care Forgot.

Chapter Sixteen

By the time we reached the eighteen-mile-long bridge spanning the Atchafalaya Swamp, Diane had downed her lunch and was snoozing in the backseat.

We'd kept the top up and turned on the air-conditioning. I held the powerful car to the speed limit, taking care to stay in the outside lane so every other vehicle on the road could pass.

And they did.

After leaving Baton Rouge on I-12, we ran into road construction, an ongoing project in Louisiana. I can't remember a time in the last thirty years I didn't run into construction on the way into New Orleans.

As I've grown older, I've tried to obey road signs, and when I spotted one stating the right lane was closed a mile head and I was to move to the left lane, I did. Sure enough, after half a mile, cars started slowing. Dutifully, I fell in at the rear. But naturally, there were those idiots passing us on the right to see how far they could get before breaking into line.

I stayed in my place in the line of vehicles, careful not to leave more than ten or twelve feet between me and the car ahead. I discovered years ago, if you leave fifteen feet, a twenty-foot car will try to pull in. Must be a macho sort of thing. Or a death wish.

To my delight, a massive eighteen-wheeler a few cars back pulled out into the right lane, effectively blocking it so the jerks couldn't sneak in ahead of us.

Road signs in Louisiana usually warn you thirty seconds after you could have taken an exit that would have permitted you to avoid the traffic jam.

This time, the road sign was correct.

By three o'clock, we were comfortably ensconced in rooms next door to each other at the Lafitte Courtyard on Chartres Street, a few blocks south of Jackson Square in the French Quarter. One block over and three or four north on Royal was Jimmy Ramsey's haunted house.

I'd experienced enough of New Orleans that it no longer held any magic or mystery for me. Without a doubt, it is a world strikingly different from that which the average tourist visits, but most never peer into the underbelly of that world, which is mostly seedy and filled with greed and selfishness.

Drugs were rampant, muggings common, thefts invariable, and scams without end.

To the uninitiated, it was all glitter and glamour. To the initiated, it reeked of depravity.

Slipping into fresh clothes after showering, I booted my laptop and pulled up my mail. To my delight, Eddie Dyson had responded.

I skimmed his reply but was disappointed to find he had not provided information on Benoit's cell mates. Technical problems, he had explained, which really meant nothing to me. Still, I had some answers. I set up my small portable printer and made a hard copy.

The only additional details of the heist Eddie could provide that I hadn't already learned from Louis Brasseaux and Emerente Landry at the *Priouxville Bayou News* or from Oscar Mouton at the Bayou car lot was that Theriot hit the Eloi Saint Julian Jewelers on July 6, and every single lead the law came up with ran into a dead end.

According to Eddie, Jimmy Ramsey lost almost a quarter million in shaky investments and was reduced to his teacher retirement income of thirty-six thousand dollars annually. I paused to study the last statement. Ramsey had over thirty years in the business. His retirement should have been considerably more, unless he took part of it out as a lump sum.

Besides, if he'd lost all his savings, how could he afford a three-story brick in the French Quarter? Of course there was the profit he had from the sale of his place on Ghost Bayou. On the other hand, I had no idea how much he'd owed on the house or how much he had cleared.

One thing I knew for sure, the prices of French Quarter multi-story structures were counted off by the millions, not thousands. Leaning back in my chair, I decided those were some of the questions I wanted answers to.

Around four o'clock, I rang Diane. I wanted to pay Jimmy Ramsey a visit, and I was not too keen about leaving her by herself. I didn't figure we'd have any trouble, for, other than Jack, no one knew we were here. Still, I'd learned long ago not to take anything for granted.

She answered on the fourth ring, her voice slurred with sleep. She begged off, swearing her door was locked and the safety chain fastened.

We were on the third floor, and our balconies overlooked a lush patio. "What about the balcony doors?"

"Them too."

Reluctantly, I agreed to go alone, hoping I wouldn't regret my decision.

A few clouds had rolled in from the south, casting welcome shadows over the Quarter. I headed west down Toulouse to Royal and turned right. Despite the cloud cover, heat radiated from the sidewalk. All saloon and bar doors were thrown wide open, their dark interiors inviting sweltering tourists into their cool depths.

A few blocks north, I halted on the sidewalk and looked up at Ramsey's three-story house, the Dupre House, a brownstone edifice shrouded by the infamy that came from the savage torture of servants in the 1840s.

Growing up in rural Louisiana, I had listened on raw winter nights around the fireplace to Grand-père Moise telling stories he had heard while selling his sweet potatoes and other goods in the French Market.

One of the most chilling stories was of the Dupre House, and of its mistress, Madame Dupre, and her treatment of her servants.

Even if such a person did exist, the last hundred and seventy years offered so much embellishment that fiction and fact had become so mixed, neither could be discerned.

On the second floor of the brownstone was a covered gallery surrounded by a wrought-iron railing of fleurs-de-lis, accessed by a flight of stairs at either end.

Next to the large oak door on the gallery was a sign:

> TOURS — 8 PM; 10 PM
> ADULTS — $20.00
> 12 AND UNDER — $7.00

I knocked on the door.

No answer.

I knocked again.

Moments later, the door opened and a paunchy man with thinning hair and a bulbous nose stared at me. "Yes?"

"My name's Tony Boudreaux. I'm looking for Jimmy Ramsey. I was told he owns this house."

The older man, who was about my height, studied me suspiciously. "What about?"

I took a step back. "You're Mr. Ramsey?" I could see the wheels spinning in his head.

With a look of dismissal on his face, he growled, "If you're selling anything, I'm not buying." He started to close the door.

"The only thing I'm selling, Mr. Ramsey, is a share of a two-million-dollar reward."

The door swung back open. An expression of understanding played over his plump face and then faded into amused tolerance.

"The diamonds, huh?" He shook his head. "Nobody's found them yet." It was a statement, not a question.

"Nope. Not yet. That's what I wanted to talk to you about."

"Boudreaux, huh? You a cop?"

"Plain citizen. A friend of mine bought your old house on Ghost Bayou. Someone worked him over trying to find the diamonds."

"So?"

"So, I figured on trying my hand at running them down. There's still a 25 percent reward for the return of the loot."

A faint smile played over his lips as if he were harboring a secret. He glanced at his watch and then pushed the screen open. "I wouldn't mind talking about the diamonds again. It's been years. Come on in. I was just getting ready to relax out on the patio with an ice-cold mint julep. How does that sound to you?"

"I'm your man," I replied, stepping through the open door and following Ramsey out back, noting how his bulk forced him to swing his arms and legs wide when he waddled.

He pointed through another screen. "There's the garden. Go on out. I'll make us some drinks."

The yard was about a thirty-by-thirty square enclosed with the same faded red bricks as the surrounding buildings. In front of the walls grew bougainvillea. Lush flowers in myriad reds and yellows and pinks sprouted in profusion in the beds along all four walls, their pleasant aromas hanging heavy in the humid air.

In the middle of the garden was a red-tiled patio with a fish-pond in the middle. Various species of goldfish swam in the clear water.

I stood watching them until I heard the screen close.

Ramsey gestured to one of the cushioned patio chairs in the shade and placed the tray with the pitcher of mint juleps and glasses on the garden table beside the chair.

He poured a glass and handed it to me, then poured his own and eased down into the chair across from the round garden table. Sipping his drink, he leaned back in his chair. "All right now, Mr. Boudreaux. Let's talk about the diamonds."

I sipped the mint julep. It was light on the julep, which was fine with me. The minty-flavored water was ice cold and refreshing. "Delicious."

"I've always preferred them light." He squinted up at the blue sky and the bright sunlight cutting a slash across the top floor of the adjoining building. "Never really liked straight whiskey on hot days. In winter, when the rain is icy and the wind miserable, straight whiskey is fine." He sipped his drink. "But you didn't come here to talk about mint juleps."

I leaned forward. "No. The diamonds that Al Theriot and the Judice boys heisted here in New Orleans. You remember Theriot?"

"How could I forget him? I bought his place on the bayou back in—" He paused and frowned. "I don't remember exactly when, but it was the mid-nineties."

"And then you sold it to Big Tim Strollo five or six years later, right?"

He looked at me in surprise and, with a wry edge to his voice, remarked, "You've done your homework, I see."

"I try. You know some diamonds turned up a few years later, I suppose?"

He suppressed a laugh. "I heard about that. Talk about a kick in the head."

"Oh?" I leaned forward. "How's that?"

He paused, studying me for a few moments as if he were trying to decide what to say next. "What if I told you Al Theriot and me had planned the heist?"

Chapter Seventeen

Over the years, I've dealt with individuals from just about every stratum of society, from homeless winos in back alleys to aristocratic snobs who believe they're better than the rest of the world. I've managed to fashion a fairly tight rein on my emotions, remaining impassive, at least on the outside, to elicit as much information as possible.

My resolve failed me at his announcement. "You—you what?"

"Well, maybe *planned* isn't the best word when you get right down to it, but Al and I talked about the job." He paused. "You know, for you to run me down over here tells me you're not one of those muscle-bound bozos with sawdust for brains."

I shrugged, wondering if he meant that as a compliment.

He continued. "Obviously, you've carried out quite a bit of research back in Priouxville, so you're bound to know that I sold out to Strollo because of financial reverses." He paused, staring at me, his eyes questioning.

"I might have heard something about it," I replied.

"Oh, yeah. You heard. You had to. And if you're as smart as I figure, you probably think the diamonds are how I got this place here."

"Well, it does make a person wonder."

"I bet. Anyway, Al and I hit it off when we first met. That was a couple years earlier, when I had leased a cabin farther down on the bayou. Then I bought his place when he hit hard times. Later, he came to me wanting money to pay off some gambling debts. By then I'd lost three quarters of my own investments. So we started looking around for alternatives. In other words," he added, "the heist."

Shifting his bulk in the cushioned chair, Ramsey chuckled. "Later, when I was by myself, I realized just what a stupid idea it was, so I backed out. But not Al. He was determined to go through with it. He'd even lined up a fence in Baton Rouge."

He saw the question on my face. "No, I didn't ask, and he didn't tell me who it was. Said I was better off not knowing. After that, he never mentioned the job again. I kept telling myself he'd forgotten about it. I suppose that's what I wanted to believe." He paused to down the rest of his drink and gestured to mine. "You're not drinking."

"Huh? Oh. Fascinating story," I remarked, taking a long sip of the libation, not only because it was refreshing, but also because I needed a stiff drink after his announcement.

Pouring himself another, Ramsey continued. "You believe in luck, Mr. Boudreaux?"

"Bad luck, yeah. Good luck? Not much. Why?"

"Well, I imagine that's how old Al felt. You see, luck or fate, or whatever you want to call it, stepped in and threw him a wicked curve. He had made arrangements to meet the fence after the heist. On the way to the meeting, the fence was killed in a car wreck on the interstate. And there was Al, stuck with eight million dollars in diamonds hotter than old Satan's barbecue pit."

"So that's why he hid them?"

"Yeah. I was visiting family over in Texas when the news broke that Eloi Saint Julian's had been hit. It was on every TV channel and radio station. Well, when I returned two or three days later, Al was waiting for me at the house."

"Your place?"

"Yeah. The one I'd bought from him. Oh, we were good friends. Both confirmed bachelors. From time to time over the years, we'd have a fish fry or barbecue at his place or mine. Even after I bought his house, we kept partying together. You know, that sort of thing. He was a real personable guy."

He hesitated, then continued his story. "I could tell he was worried. He said the Judice brothers went back home after the heist as if nothing had happened. In fact, they had reported to work at the local fish house the next morning. He'd already hidden the diamonds. That's when he told me about the fence."

Ramsey paused and shook his head. "You know, he really believed they'd pulled it off. Masks, gloves, stolen car, two of them were in and out of the jewelry store in ninety seconds. The car waited at the curb. Five minutes later, they switched cars out in the Ninth Ward. You know the Ninth?"

"Do I? Those old boys can strip a car in thirty seconds out there. I'm surprised their getaway car was in one piece."

"That was where they fouled up. Al paid an old boy to keep it safe. He broke under questioning. All he could tell the cops was the make, model, and color, but that's all they needed."

I drained my glass and refilled it from the pitcher. "How long did it take?"

"Before the cops nailed him?"

"Yeah."

"Longer than I expected. About six months or so. From what I heard, the Judice boys dodged the law for five or six years. They might have beat the statute of limitations, but one of them got drunk and talked."

Donat Judice, I told myself.

Overhead, the evening clouds took on a golden sheen from the setting sun. I glanced around the small, snug garden, a perfect refuge from the bustling world beyond. "He never mentioned the diamonds again?"

"A couple of days before they nailed him. He'd dropped by my place. From the way he acted, he knew his string had just about run out. That was when he told me he had split the loot and hidden it in two different spots."

"That was the last you saw of him?"

"Oh, no. I visited him two or three times before he got himself killed. Kind of hated not to, you know? I'd be sitting there, looking through the glass at him, and thinking, 'Man, that could be me rotting away in there.' You know what I mean?"

Chuckling, I replied, "Yeah. I know."

"Did he ever say anything else about the diamonds?"

Ramsey looked up at me. "One time. He told me he'd arranged to fence some of the diamonds to pay a lawyer to spring him. He begged me to get the diamonds. I refused at first, but by then, I knew I was going to have to get rid of the house. I was running out of money. So I agreed."

I sat forward in the cushioned chair. "How much was he talking about?"

Ramsey shrugged. "I don't know. I never got them." When he saw my frown, he continued. "Two days later, he was dead. I left the diamonds alone. I didn't want the hassle of answering all kinds of questions and perhaps being charged as an accessory. I had a cousin who lived in Priouxville, K. D. Dople. He's dead now, but he'd spent a lot of time out at the house. I made the mistake of telling him about the jewels. A few days later, he got nailed for burglary and spent time in jail. As soon as he got out, him and an old boy by the name of Lester Percher just up and vanished from the parish. Then some of the diamonds showed up in a pawnshop in Alexandria." He snorted. "Idiots probably didn't get even ten cents on the dollar."

I whistled softly, thinking of Lester Percher's shrimp boat. "You're probably right," I said. "What happened to Dople?"

"Whacked."

"They ever find out who did it?"

"Nah. Sheriff Lacoutrue of Priouxville had asked me about K. D. after the jewels turned up. He figured Lester or K. D. might be mixed up in it, since both of them had left town." He paused. "Neither of them had what you could call a sterling reputation around there."

I shook my head. "Those were the diamonds hidden in the wall of one of the service bays at the car lot, right?"

He stared at me in disbelief. "How—"

"Percher."

"You found him?"

"Yep. He's like a clam," I lied. I couldn't see what good it would do to tell him of Lester's shrimp boat. The whole situation was confused enough. No sense in muddying the water any further.

"Can't say I blame him," he said, amused.

"Now, what was it you were saying?"

"Well, Lacoutrue even checked on my finances. Like you, he probably wondered if I used the diamonds to help get into this place."

"Well, Mr. Ramsey, you have to admit, the situation does warrant the question."

"I understand that. I take it you didn't check back through parish records. If you had, you'd have seen that Al's old man paid the Prioux family thirty thousand for the place. When Al got the place, he put a bundle into it. I paid a hundred thousand, and Strollo—" Lowering his voice, he continued, "Strollo didn't care what he spent. It was Mafia money anyway. He paid two hundred. I came over here with just enough down payment to get into this place."

I thought I already knew the answer to the next question that had been nagging at me, but I wanted to hear it from him. "With a superintendent's retirement, you should have been able to stay on the bayou."

He laughed, and to give him credit, his ears turned red with embarrassment. "I messed up when I retired. I thought I knew all about investing, so I took only a third in annuities. The rest I took in a lump sum that I invested, planning on making a million bucks."

In a way, I felt sorry for the guy. "It happens."

He reached for the pitcher. "Looks like we need a refill."

I begged off. "No more for me, thanks."

"You sure?"

"Positive." I remembered Emerente and Brasseaux over at the *Priouxville Bayou News* talking about how picky Theriot had been in the reconstruction of the house. "You say Theriot put a bundle into building the place?"

"Yeah."

"I heard he was real particular about it."

He shrugged as he poured himself another mint julep. "I

heard the same thing. I can tell you, and you probably noticed if you've been at the place, the workmen did a beautiful job. Of course, to be honest, why he wanted to fit old railings and balusters from the original home onto the stairs puzzled me. If I'd stayed, I would have replaced them."

"I thought I was the only one who had noticed," I said.

"An eyesore, huh? But that was part of the deal. I had to keep them or turn back the house. Nutty, huh? After he got killed, I just forgot about the railings." He sipped his drink and held up the glass to me. "Sure you don't want another?"

I shook my head. I rose and glanced around. "You must have a pretty good business."

"Not bad. I rent the place out for horror films four or five times a years. Pays the mortgage. With my Social Security, what's left of my teacher retirement, and the tours, I manage."

I extended my hand. "Thanks for the time."

"No problem. I enjoyed it."

He led the way back through the house.

"One other thing," I said. "L. Q. Benoit. You know him?"

He glanced over his shoulder. "The town thief. Yeah. He's sneaky, nosy as sin. He and his pals are like leeches. They grab everything that isn't nailed down."

"His pals? You mean Primeaux and Vitale?"

He nodded. "Yeah. That's them. Wouldn't trust any of them any farther than I could throw this house."

"They're all dead," I replied.

"Dead?" Then he snorted. "Well, it doesn't surprise me. Someone was bound to run them down or shoot them. Like I said, they were no good." He opened the front door. "Just a minute." He fumbled in his shirt pocket and handed me a ticket. "Why don't you take the tour tonight? On me."

I took the proffered ticket. "Can you spare another? I've got a friend."

"Sure. Here you go."

I paused on the gallery outside the front door and looked around. Dusk had settled over the city. The narrow streets and cracked sidewalks were growing crowded with tourists. Lilting strains of accordions accompanied by fiddle music poured from the open doorways into the street.

The last hour or so with Jimmy Ramsey had given me nothing more than a strong feeling that he had no interest in the whereabouts of the diamonds. His story supported both Lester Percher's version of the diamonds and Dople's murder.

From what little Ramsey had said about Benoit and his drinking buddies, I was more convinced than ever that the old man had learned something about the diamonds in prison. It wasn't too much of a stretch to figure that the deaths of his two pals were for the same reason.

Someone had been convinced the two knew the location of the diamonds. In all probability, the poor drunks might have been caught in a no-win situation. The only way they could stop the beatings was if they revealed the secret of the diamonds.

Why didn't they? The only explanation was, they didn't know.

Benoit, on the other hand, probably knew. Why didn't he speak up, unless he knew he was dead anyway?

When I turned the corner off Royal onto Toulouse, I glimpsed a long-haired man dart into a passageway halfway down the block. For a moment, I thought I recognized him, but just as quickly I dismissed the notion. The French Quarter was full of strange-looking characters.

When I passed the passageway, I peered down it. The far end was consumed by inky darkness. I guessed a courtyard lay beyond.

A few drops of rain struck my face. I paused in front of the Lafitte Courtyard and glanced south toward Canal Street. A white veil of rain raced up the narrow street toward me. I stepped inside just as the rain struck.

Upstairs, I knocked on Diane's door.

There was no answer.

I listened closely for footsteps and knocked again.

Still no answer.

A shiver of panic ran up my spine.

Chapter Eighteen

Just as I started to beat on the door, I heard Diane call out, "Who is it?"

A thousand-pound weight slipped off my shoulders. "Me. Tony."

"Just a minute." I heard the clatter of the safety chain, and then the door opened. She smiled up at me, her eyes puffy with sleep, her short brown hair tousled.

"Sorry. I didn't mean to wake you," I muttered.

She smiled sleepily. "I was awake. I was just lying there, enjoying the peace and quiet." She stepped back and opened the door. "Come on in." She made a sweeping gesture at the living area, which had kitchen facilities, a foldout couch, a TV, and a small table. "Sorry I don't have anything to offer other than water."

"No problem. I just wanted to see if you were getting hungry."

Her eyes grew wide. "Are you kidding? That hamburger's down to my toes."

I skimmed over the details of my conversation with Jimmy Ramsey as we walked the few blocks to the Acme Oyster House on Iberville Street. Walking is the most efficient means of transportation within the French Quarter. The narrow streets allow for only a single vehicle; that's why most of the streets are one-way.

Dusk had given way to night. Tourists and revelers filled the sidewalks, unlike other sections of New Orleans, especially since Katrina. The local law was plainly visible.

The Acme, upon first glance, appeared nothing more than a hole-in-the-wall, but inside, it was jam-packed with fantastic service and even more fantastic food. A ten-star on anyone's five-star grid.

Diane ordered the oyster platter, I ordered the shrimp platter, and, as when we were married, we split our entrées with each other.

During the meal, I went into more detail about the visit with Jimmy Ramsey, and she squealed with delight when I showed her the tickets he'd given us.

"A real haunted house?" she asked, dabbing a piece of golden oyster in sauce and popping it into her mouth. "What's it like? Have I heard about it?"

"I don't know." I shrugged, and around a bite of shrimp, I explained. "The madame of the house was named Dupre. She'd married a count or something back in the early 1800s. Story is, she tortured her servants, and they came back to haunt her."

"Why didn't someone do something about it? The law? They had the law back then, didn't they?"

"Her husband was too influential. When asked about it, he just brushed it off. He was too important for the law to dispute his word. Anyway, a couple of years later, the house burned. That's when the Dupres' secret came out."

Diane stared at me, her fork poised in midair, a bite-sized chunk of golden oyster motionless on the tines. "So, what then?"

"A local judge watching the fire heard screams from inside. When he asked Dupre if there were people inside, Dupre rebuffed him. Later that night the Dupres disappeared. While inspecting the building the next morning, city officials discovered charred bodies."

Wide-eyed, she stared at me. "What about the Dupres?"

"Gone. They still had friends in New Orleans. That's how they got their money out. Legend has it, they sailed to Barbados, where they continued carrying out their savage tortures."

Diane shivered, then popped the oyster between her lips. "Creepy. I don't know if I want to go there or not."

"It's just old stories, embellished over the years. She probably slapped a servant once, and the story grew from there."

By the time we left the Acme, it was almost seven. We headed toward Bourbon Street. "If we hurry," I said, "we can catch the eight o'clock tour at the Dupre House."

Diane made a face. "Let's take the later one." She gestured at all the bright lights of Bourbon Street. "I want to play tourist. Maybe get a drink or two." She linked her arm through mine and laid her head on my shoulder. "Okay?"

"Okay," I replied reluctantly, remembering San Antonio. "Maybe just one."

Bourbon Street was jumping. Of course, it's always jumping, and as the night grows older, it jumps even higher. The first couple of blocks, we just ambled along, pausing to glance inside the open doors that screamed, "Come in, sinner, come in, come in."

We found a corner bar with folding doors opening onto the sidewalk. For the next thirty minutes, we each nursed our vodka Collins and watched the crowds pass. I grew a little antsy when she asked for another.

Sometime later, I spotted an empty carriage. Grabbing Diane by the arm, I exclaimed, "Come on. Let's take a carriage ride."

It was a little two-bench surrey with fringe, pulled by an ancient mule that knew every turn on his route. For the next thirty minutes we toured the Quarter, ending up at Jackson Square right across from the Café du Monde, where we dunked beignets in some of the best coffee ever brewed.

I glanced at my watch. Almost ten. "Time to go," I announced, pushing back from the table and offering her my hand.

The artists, fortune-tellers, and Tarot card readers were still out along the esplanade around Jackson Square, all clamoring for our attention as we passed.

The next block over, we turned on Royal Street and ten minutes later climbed the stairs to the front door of the Dupre house.

Counting Diane and me, there were fifteen tourists standing about in the shadowy foyer, illumined only by half a dozen flickering candles.

I looked around for Ramsey, but the paunchy man was nowhere to be seen. Moments later, a slender figure in black entered, wearing a sweeping cape. In the dim light, his sallow face stood out in sharp contrast to his shoulder-length black hair and clothing.

He introduced himself as Pierre, a grandson six times removed from the Count and Madame Dupre. His first order of business was collecting tickets and, in some instances, cash.

I did some fast figuring in my head. Fifteen suckers at twenty bucks a head for two tours added up to six hundred a night. Not bad, not bad, not bad.

Maybe there was something to be said for the haunting business.

Holding a guttering candle at chest level so the shadows cast his face in eerie relief, Pierre quickly gave us the background of his ancestors before leading us into an adjoining room, replete with manacles hanging from two walls, and a cat-o'-nine-tails on another. Along one wall and floor were gruesome stains, purportedly the blood of those who had been held there, stains that continued, even after two hundred years, to resist all efforts to remove them.

Shivering, Diane wrapped both her arms around my right arm as we ascended a flight of stairs.

At the top, our guide pointed out a series of slab doors, each with a tiny window through which one could see a small cubicle.

Muted groans and shivers emanated from the tourists.

Diane stood on tiptoe and whispered in my ear, "This gives me the creeps."

I squeezed her hand. "Me too."

Slowly, the curious tourists filed by the cubicles, mumbling soft "ohs" and "ahs" as they passed.

In the next room dangled four nooses. In a low, macabre voice, our guide whispered, "The fire that consumed my ancestors' home permitted the populace of New Orleans to witness horrors beyond description."

Amid an undercurrent of apprehensive gasps, the crowd of tourists shrank away from the nooses. I saw a glitter of amusement in our guide's eyes.

And then in a swift, sharp move, he spun to face us, pulling his cape up over his lips. He glared at us in a manner that reminded me of old Bela Lugosi movies. With a black-gloved hand, he pointed to a door at the top of a flight of stairs. "But nothing," he hissed, "drove terror into the city's bones as much as the next room to which you will bear witness."

Chapter Nineteen

The door at the top of the stairs opened onto a candlelit balcony overlooking a chamber two floors below. High above, a large chandelier with dim lights replicating guttering candles cast gloomy shadows over the room.

Below, floodlights illumined a macabre torture chamber like something out of a medieval castle. A collective gasp filled the room, followed by a brief soliloquy from our guide elaborating on the scene.

A walkway spanned the chamber, leading from our balcony to another on the far wall. Speaking softly among themselves, the crowd began filing across, a few pausing to study the chilling scene below.

Diane and I brought up the rear.

Just before she and I reached the far side, I heard a hissing sound. I glanced up and spotted the enormous chandelier hurtling toward us. I lunged forward, slamming my hand into Diane's back and knocking her forcibly into the crowd. The chandelier struck, and the walkway began to fall. I made a frantic leap for the railing on the perimeter of the balcony.

My fingers wrapped around one of the carved balusters, swinging me forward into the wall as the fixture and the walkway smashed into the chamber below. Moments later, grasping fingers clutched my wrist, hauling me to safety.

Diane and I remained on the third landing as the guide hastily led the rest of the tourists downstairs and outside before returning.

The only light was from below, casting the third-floor landing in misshapen shadows. Gasping for breath, Jimmy Ramsey clambered up the stairs and hurried across the balcony and flipped on a light, which didn't disperse the shadows to any great degree. He shook his head slowly as he looked around, his face taut with concern. "I'm just glad no one got hurt."

"Not half as glad as I am," I replied, standing beside him on the balcony, inspecting the damage. Diane linked her arm through mine. I picked up the cable securing the chandelier to the ceiling. It had not been cut; it had slipped loose. I showed it to Ramsey. "What happened?"

"Somehow the cable came loose," Ramsey said to Pierre.

I glanced at Pierre and then back at Ramsey. "'Somehow'?"

The guide, an aging offspring of 1960s flower children, shook his head. "I don't know how, Jimmy. I changed the lights before the first tour, but I put the cable back and locked it."

"'Locked it'?" I frowned at Ramsey.

He motioned for us to follow. "I'll show you."

He pointed out a two-pronged cleat and a heavy metal plate, each bolted to the wall next to a door. A curved shackle extended a few inches from the plate. On the floor was a combination lock, the shackle of which was still locked.

Ramsey cursed. "Would you look at this?" He picked up the lock and stared at Pierre in disbelief. "You left the lock off."

Pierre shook his head emphatically. "No way. No way at all. I tell you, Jimmy, I locked that thing. I swear I locked it."

I studied the lock in Ramsey's hand. It was a combination lock. I held out my hand. "Let me see it." I turned it over in my hand, inspecting it. "This is the lock you used?"

"Yeah." He picked up an end of the loose cable and made a slipknot in it. "After we raise the chandelier, we wrap the cable around the cleat several times, and then make a slipknot in the cable. We lock the slipknot to the shackle on the plate with this padlock." He paused. "It can't come loose. It's impossible. Someone did it on purpose. Someone wanted the chandelier to fall."

I felt Diane's manicured nails dig into my arm, but to her credit, she kept her feelings to herself. I nodded to the door beside the cleat. "Where does that door go?"

"It's a back stairway down to the foyer."

"Could someone have used it?"

Ramsey shrugged. "I suppose, but how would they get in?"

Glancing at Pierre, I asked, "Do you take a head count of the tours?"

"Sure," he said, looking over at Ramsey. "You know, to make sure I got the tickets to match the customers."

"I mean afterward."

"No." He hesitated and apologetically added, "I never saw any use for that."

"Chances are, that's how whoever it was got in. Came on the first tour, slipped away, and hid in the stairway."

Ramsey shook his head in disbelief. "But why? What did he have in mind? And how did he get the cable loose? The lock is still locked."

With Diane clinging to my arm, I opened the door to the back stairs and scanned the floor but failed to see the object for which I was searching.

Ramsey stared at the landing above the flight of stairs. "What are you looking for?"

I glanced around and spotted a light switch on the wall. The dim bulb was only a few watts brighter than the light spilling through the open door.

"It isn't here."

Diane frowned up at me. "What?"

Holding on to the combination lock, I replied, "Let's go downstairs, and I'll show you."

Ramsey cocked his head to one side. "Show us what?"

"You'll see."

Downstairs, I asked for an empty soft-drink can, which Ramsey, though puzzled, provided without comment. While I used kitchen shears to cut a rectangle about an inch and a half by an inch from the can, I explained. "I've got a hunch Pierre's right. Someone dropped the chandelier deliberately."

Ramsey shook his head. "I don't see how."

I held up the rectangle. "That's what I'm going to show you." I proceeded to cut the slip of aluminum into the shape of an M, after which I folded the legs up, leaving a V-shaped piece of aluminum with two horizontal arms. "There's an old saying, 'There never was a horse that couldn't be rode and never a man who couldn't be throwed.' Same thing here. There was never a lock that couldn't be hacked."

Folding the strip of aluminum around one leg of the curved shackle, I pressed the shackle into the lock, slipping the point of the V down into the narrow space between the body of the lock and the leg of the shackle. The V slid between the lock pin within the body of the lock and the leg. Then I simply wrapped the aluminum arms around the shackle, jiggled the V up and down, and gave a sharp yank on the shackle. It popped loose.

Pierre stared in disbelief. "How—"

I handed Ramsey the lock. "That's how he did it."

All the rotund man could do was shake his head. Finally, he managed to ask, "But why?"

I glanced at Diane. I knew why, but I decided to keep it to myself for the time being. Besides, now I had two questions to consider. Who knew we were here, and how did they learn of it? Only three of us knew: Jack, Diane, and me. "Beats me."

After the close call with the chandelier, I was reluctant to take the sidewalks back to our motel. While Royal Street was fairly well lit, Toulouse was steeped in darkness. A whole regiment could be swept from the street into a side room without anyone noticing.

The Quarter's sidewalks might still be crowded, but most of the boisterous celebrants were so drunk they couldn't see, or so consumed with passion they only had one object in mind, or so stoned they wouldn't care.

I called a cab.

During the ride to the hotel, I began to wonder if there was more going on than just the diamonds. The falling chandelier could have killed someone. That was a lot different than a bar fight or a snake in the living room.

We reached the hotel just before midnight, and the French Quarter showed no signs of slowing down. During the ride, Diane asked several questions about the events of the evening.

As much as I hated to worry her, I knew I couldn't keep the truth from her, at least part of the truth.

"I can't shake the feeling," I said, "that someone is afraid I'm going to find the diamonds."

Diane cleared her throat. "Who would be afraid you'd find the diamonds? There's got to be more than what you've told me."

I pointed to the hotel. "Let's get a nightcap, and I'll tell you."

I was fairly honest with her. I didn't mention any of the murders or the assassinations in prison. I didn't mention the snake in the house. Instead, I put the snake in my pickup. I told her about the prowlers and about the trip to Cocodrie Slough.

"Now, all of these are probably just coincidences, including the chandelier," I said in an effort to assuage any fears. "Those diamonds are valuable. A lot of people know about them. I don't care about the diamonds as much as I do finding those jokers who whipped on your husband."

Smiling gratefully, she leaned forward and rested her hand on mine. "Thanks, Tony, for looking after Jack."

I saw the sincerity in her eyes and heard it in her voice. Maybe she wasn't coming on to me. Maybe I was too full of myself. I shrugged. "No problem."

After I climbed into bed, the phone rang. It was Diane. "I just wanted to thank you again for trying to find those who hurt Jack. I know that it is awkward for both of us, having been married, but I'm very grateful to you. You're a good friend."

"Thanks. I'll find them. Don't worry. And—who knows?— maybe we'll stumble across the diamonds at the same time."

Later, as I lay staring at the ceiling upon which lights from the streets below reflected, I tried to fit the pieces of the last few days together.

The diamonds were still out there, and someone wanted them badly, so badly that, when you tossed in Jack's beating, the snake in the house, Cocodrie Slough, and the falling chandelier, the whole scenario took a decidedly violent turn.

To go to so much trouble, someone was determined to have the jewels. And who could blame 'em? I'm no expert on jewels, but I couldn't help assuming that eight million in gems thirteen years ago could have doubled in value by today.

Whoever was trying to drive me away from the diamonds must know just how to get rid of them. Such a transaction called for someone who possessed more than just a passing acquaintance with the detailed intricacies of moving stolen diamonds, an almost impossible task without accompanying papers.

I had no idea who I was up against, but he, or she, was no one I could afford to take lightly.

Usually in working a case, you can narrow your list of suspects by learning who has the most to gain. In this case, that was everyone.

Chapter Twenty

I rolled over onto my side, but sleep failed to come. And the clamor from the streets below didn't help. So much for the wisdom of booking a hotel in the middle of the French Quarter.

At two A.M., I sat up and turned on the TV. If I'd had a drink around, I would have taken one or two, but for the last few weeks, except for our misadventure at Cocodrie Slough and a couple of weak drinks today, I'd been pretty much a teetotaler.

Although I was a long-term member of AA, it was not because I was addicted to alcohol. I know, I know, that's what all drunks say, but it never bothered me to quit. And I'm not going to make the old joke that "I'd quit a thousand times" either. It was merely a habit, but, in all fairness, I guess you could say it was also a crutch I used to fill extra time.

Back in my apartment, I have beer and wine in the refrigerator; bourbon, gin, vodka, and rum in the cabinet; and mixers under the sink.

None has been opened in over six months.

I've seen alcohol ruin too many lives—and not just the drunk's, but also his or her family's. That isn't fair to anyone.

I stared, unseeing, at the TV, letting the case of the hidden diamonds ruminate in my brain. I got to thinking about T-Ball from Charenton showing up in Cocodrie Slough, wondering where he'd picked up such a nickname. I didn't know about the Ball, but the *T* didn't fit; in the French Cajun vernacular, the prefix *T* signifies small. I finally concluded that perhaps it was just a result of perverted humor, like a fat person picking up the nickname Skinny.

That night on the ride back from Cocodrie Slough after our brouhaha with the village's finest, the fact that the Naquins had wondered what T-Ball was doing there had given me the impression he usually stuck pretty close to home—and his horses.

Next thing I knew, sunlight filtered through the closed curtains and the morning news blared on the TV.

The phone rang. It was Diane. She was already dressed and ready for breakfast. "I'll be right over," she announced when I said I was still in bed. "Put your coffee on. I'll have a cup while you hurry up and dress. Unlock the door for me."

After the last twenty-four hours together, I'd dismissed the San Antonio incident, but her announcement resurrected my concern. Maybe I wasn't so full of myself.

I turned on the coffee, grabbed a change of clothes, and retreated to the bathroom.

Moments later, she called from the living room, "I'm here."

"Make yourself comfortable. The coffee should be ready."

After showering and shaving, I slipped into washed-out jeans and a polo shirt. I padded barefoot into the bedroom for socks and my running shoes.

From the corner of my eye, I spotted movement. I looked around. Diane watched me from the doorway, a cup of coffee in her hand. She wore cream-colored slacks and a matching blouse. "The years have been good to you," she said, her eyes appraising me.

Ever the Southern gallant, I replied, "I can say the same for you."

Her cheeks colored, and her eyes shone. "You're just saying that."

"You know me better than that. You always did take care of yourself."

Her eyes lost their focus as they gazed into the past. "We did have some good times, didn't we?"

That was the fastest I'd ever tied my shoes. "Yeah. What times we weren't fighting."

She laughed and turned back to the living room. "Hurry up. I'm starving."

Downstairs, the hotel served a buffet breakfast with enough choices to give anyone pause in deciding just which entrée to enjoy.

Back in Austin, breakfast is usually an afterthought, but I was like a kid in a candy store when I stood before that buffet of steaming eggs, omelets, sausage, bacon, pancakes, hash browns, grits, gravy, biscuits, toast, cereals, and fruit.

I considered serving myself a small portion of everything, but that would be way too much, so I opted for scrambled eggs, grits, gravy, and one biscuit.

Over an after-breakfast cup of coffee, Diane asked about our plans for the day.

"Head back home," I replied. "Soon as we can."

She smiled with relief. "Good." Her smile grew shy. "I miss that hardheaded husband of mine."

Back in my room, I sat on the edge of the bed and booted up my laptop and searched for a Wi-Fi connection to check my e-mail. Eddie Dyson had finally found some information concerning L. Q. Benoit's cell mates. I stiffened upon reading Eddie's report. Benoit's cell mates had been Billy Arsenault from Alexandria; C. K. Judice from Charenton; and Paul Foret from Monroe.

My heart thudded in my chest when I saw the name C. K. Judice. Benoit had been one of his cell mates. Whether Judice revealed the location of the diamonds to Benoit or not was up for grabs, but at least the possibility now existed.

Pulling out my three-by-five note cards, I thumbed through them to the information Sheriff Lacoutrue had provided. He had given me four names: Billy Arsenault from Alexandria; Donald Carson of New Orleans; Paul Foret from Monroe; and John Boneau from Branch. No C. K. Judice!

Pursing my lips thoughtfully, I leaned back and examined the information on the screen, wondering about the difference in the two lists. If I had to wager a bet on which of the two was more accurate, I'd go with Eddie. He's expensive, but his information has always been worth it.

Rising from the bed, I stared out the glass doors separating the small balcony from the bedroom. Why the discrepancy?

The jangling of the phone interrupted my thoughts.

Diane was ready. I quickly saved my information to the hard drive and then the flash drive, which I stuck in my pocket.

We refueled at a convenience store on the west side of Lee Circle on St. Charles before heading out later that morning. The sun was a molten ball in a clear blue sky, so we left the top up to take advantage of the air-conditioning.

I-10 as usual was under construction, forcing vehicles into a few lanes, thus slowing traffic. After several minutes of thirty-mile-per-hour boredom, traffic began to speed up, and soon we were moving along well above the limit.

Some miles out, I-10 spans the southern reaches of Lake Pont-chartrain. A few boats, which appeared to be crabbers, bobbed in the shallow waters near the shoreline.

Diane had called Jack before we left and was filling me in on the details of their conversation. He was doing well, and the doctors planned on releasing him the next day. She beamed at me. "It'll be so nice to have him back home."

Before I could agree, the engine sputtered, then backfired and died.

I exclaimed, "What the—?" The steering wheel almost froze. I felt like I was driving a tank when I steered the Cadillac to the narrow safety zone next to the concrete railing.

We rolled to a halt. For a moment, I just stared at the gauges.

To our left, trucks and cars whizzed by, each one rocking the Cadillac as it blasted past. Diane gasped, "What happened?"

As a teenager, I'd worked on cars. Today? Forget it. I seldom open the hood any longer. Whenever I do, I haven't the remotest idea what I'm observing other than tubes and wires going in every direction. "Beats me." I shoved the transmission into park and tried to start the engine. Nothing, not even a tiny click. I leaned back and muttered a curse.

With a trace of alarm, Diane spoke up. "Tony! What are we going to do?"

"We're going to call for help, that's what," I replied, pulling out my cell. I muttered a curse. "No signal."

"Now what?"

"Try yours."

She did, with the same result.

I pointed down the interstate. "There's an emergency phone down there. They'll send out some help."

Although I knew it would be an exercise in futility, I popped open the hood and stared at the tangle of wires. I suppose I was hoping to spot a sign and arrow pointing out the problem. I studied the tangle for about five minutes. All I accomplished was wasting five minutes.

With a shrug, I headed for the emergency phone.

A short time later, I climbed back into the car. "The cavalry's on the way," I said.

"How long, do you figure?"

I rolled my eyes. "Who knows? Probably an hour at least."

We settled back for a long wait.

To our surprise, a bright red tow truck with the sign NEW OR-LEANS TOWING on the doors pulled up only a few minutes later. Two guys jumped out. The driver, a short pudgy guy, wore dirty overalls. His helper wore jeans and a T-shirt with NEW ORLEANS OR BUST on the front.

"That was fast," I said, opening the door.

"Yeah. We happened to be out on the road," the driver replied. While he introduced himself as Buzz and his helper as Turk, the latter peered under the hood, fiddling with whatever you fiddle with.

Turk lifted his eyes and caught my gaze. "Give it a try."

I turned the ignition.

Still nothing.

Turk pushed away from the car and closed the hood. "Can't do nothing here, Buzz."

Buzz scratched his short hair. "Sorry we can't get you up and going, folks." He gestured west on I-10. "We'll tow you on up to Frenier. That's where we're from. We'll take good care of you there."

Diane and I exchanged disappointed looks. I shrugged. "Maybe it won't take too long to fix."

As we rolled into Frenier, Diane picked up a signal and called Jack, telling him she'd get back with him once we learned just how long the repairs would take. She nodded as she listened to his reply. "If we have to. Don't worry."

After punching off, she looked around at me. "Jack said if it was going to take too long to repair, just to buy another car."

I shook my head. One thing about my old chum Jack Edney. Though he came into the eight million only a couple of years back, he had quickly managed to slip into the ways of the very rich with considerable ease and finesse. "Good old Jack. Impatient as always."

At Frenier Motors, which carried GM and Chrysler products, the service manager checked the Cadillac and informed us it would take only a couple of hours.

It was almost noon. "Couple hours, huh?" I looked at Diane. "Well, I don't know about you, but I'm hungry."

Diane looked surprised. "After that breakfast?"

"Yeah. How about you?"

Her growling stomach answered for her.

"I saw a cafeteria in that mall just after we turned off the interstate. Let's settle up with Buzz, and then we'll grab a cab."

When Buzz heard we were going to call a cab, he shook his head. "My van's right over there. Turk and me'll give you a ride down to the mall. Save a little after what you folks are having to put out today."

We all laughed.

The red Ford van was as shiny as the tow truck. Buzz slid open the side door. "You can sit in back here."

I helped Diane step up into the van.

She screamed. I started to look around, but an arm wrapped around my neck, and a hand pressed a rag against my mouth and nose. There was a sweet, burning taste, and the last thing I remember is being shoved through the open door into the van.

Chapter Twenty-one

I don't know how long I was unconscious, only that it was as dark as Louisiana gumbo mud when I awakened. A wave of nausea swept over me. I tried to roll off the bed, but a chain about my ankle jerked me back.

Despite the pounding in my head, I fiddled with the chain in the darkness, quickly realizing it was fastened to a manacle around my ankle, not unlike one of those we had seen in the haunted Dupre House back in New Orleans. The other end of the chain was locked around one leg of the metal bed.

I lay back, breathing hard, and looked at my watch, barely able to make out the time: three A.M. Slowly, I gathered my wits. A dim glow filled the room, and a distant boom sent faint vibrations through the house, rattling the windows. I caught a glimpse of the fading light from the flash of lightning.

Another flash, this one closer, pushed back the inky blackness of the night. Thunder rolled in, once again rattling the old house, which smelled of dust and age.

The time between the lightning and the subsequent thunder grew less and less as the spring storm approached from out of the Gulf of Mexico.

During the brief flashes of lightning, I saw I was alone. The room was furnished as a bedroom with high ceilings and strips of wallpaper falling off the walls. A dresser and chair stood along one wall; against the outside wall was an old fireplace. The grout between the bricks had crumbled. In front of it stood a potbellied stove, behind which a stovepipe ran from the floor to the ceiling.

I could only guess that meant there was also a stove on the floor directly beneath me. Trying to push away the throbbing pain in my head, I sat up on the bed. During the brilliant white explosions of lightning, I fumbled with the U-shaped manacle about my ankle. A screw pin ran through both ends of the U, and a padlock secured it through a hole in one end of the screw pin.

Inspecting the old lock, I sighed with relief. Buzz and Turk might as well have used a piece of string to fasten the manacle. All I needed was a short length of wire to hack my way free. Now I just needed to find one.

I dug through the contents in my pants pocket. I still had my flash drive, which was about the size of a pack of chewing gum, but my pocketknife was missing. Even if I had it, the blades were too large for the lock.

I looked across the room at the dresser. I could always slide the bed over to the dresser, but the scraping would sound like a bulldozer to whoever was below.

Then I remembered my cell phone. I patted my pocket and groaned. They'd taken the phone as well as the knife. I still had my wallet. Go figure.

I turned my attention to the bed. The two legs at the foot of the bed were supported by two slender tubes running horizontally from one leg to the other and secured by a weld at either end. Three evenly spaced metal tubes vertically joined the two tubes for additional support. The chain was locked around one leg between the two horizontal tubes.

Gently, I shook the tubes. They seemed solid.

Outside, a blinding flash of lightning lit the room, and the storm struck, the rain pelting the roof, rattling the windows. Blasts of wind slammed into the house. The walls emitted groans and creaks.

Excited voices echoed through the room.

I looked around, but I was still by myself.

Just before another crack of lightning deafened me, I heard the voices again, this time from the stove. *Of course,* I told myself. The common stovepipe from one stove to another acted like a telephone.

Noise would go both ways, so I tried to keep quiet as I turned back to trying to free myself. Though solidly built, the bed was old, at least seventy or eighty years. I felt the welds on the end of the horizontal tubes. There was only one way to find out how sturdy it was.

I stood beside the bed and placed a foot on the lower support and pressed hard. The weld refused to break. Next, holding the ball on top of the leg for support, I stood on the bottom tube with both feet.

Still it held.

I glanced out the window, waiting for the next bolt of lightning. Moments later, it exploded, shaking the house. I jumped up and down on the tube, and it broke away from the leg.

Voices echoed up through the stove.

Quickly, I pulled the tube back into place and looped the chain over the top rail, then placed the end of the dusty bedspread over the loose end of the bottom tube in an effort to hide it from any prying eyes. I lay back, feigning unconsciousness.

The door squeaked open. Through my closed eyelids, I saw the light from the doorway dispel some of the darkness.

"He there?" I recognized the voice as Turk's.

"Yeah," growled Buzz. "Still out."

"What was that noise, then? Sounded like someone jumping."

"It's this old house. Just a minute. I'll check him."

I held my breath as footsteps approached.

At the end of the bed, he picked up the chain I'd draped across the top support and tugged on it. "Nah. Still locked tight. Like I said, just this old house creaking."

Another bolt of lightning ripped the dark skies open, rattling the windowpanes and shaking the house.

"I don't know how those old-timers lived like this, way out in the middle of nowhere. The place is about to fall down."

"Stop your griping. Let's get back downstairs. I need a stiff drink. This rain is giving me the chills."

"What about the woman? You figure we ought to check on her?"

Buzz cursed. "She's probably still out too, but if it'll make you feel better, okay."

I lay motionless after the door closed, listening to their footsteps crossing the hall. A door squeaked open. Moments later, Buzz mumbled, "She's still out. Satisfied?"

"Yeah. Now, let's get that drink."

Their footsteps receded down the hall.

Turk called out, "These stairs are about to fall down."

Abruptly, I rolled from the bed, hoping to free the chain before they got back downstairs. I lifted the leg of the bedstead and slipped the chain from under it; then, holding the chain in my hand, I eased to the door and opened it a crack.

A dim bulb burned at one end of the hall, its pale glow barely reaching my door. I heard the two men downstairs. Moving as silently as possible, I opened each of the dresser's drawers and rifled through them.

Rain continued to pelt the house, with chain lightning performing an intermittent slashing dance across the darkness.

My fingers found a safety pin, the size once used on cloth diapers. Opening the pin, I knelt by the partially open door and quickly fit the point into the ancient padlock. Seconds later, it snapped open, and I unscrewed the locking pin in the manacle.

Voices echoed from the stove. On tiptoe, I eased across the room and opened the door in the stove's belly. The empty stove amplified their words like a loudspeaker. My blood ran cold as I eavesdropped on their conversation.

"How long you figure we'll be out here?"

Buzz grunted. "Can't tell. Just depends on what he's got in mind."

When Turk replied, there was a trace of concern in his voice. "You don't suppose he'll want us to waste them, do you?"

"All I know is, we was told to snatch them. What's the matter?" Buzz snorted. "You getting religion all of a sudden?"

"Nah. It ain't that. It's the woman. I ain't never whacked no woman."

"We wouldn't be here if you hadn't missed him with the

chandelier last night. If you'd busted him up good, maybe he would have gotten the message. He's going to keep looking. That's what he told the woman last night."

Last night! Frantically I thought back. That's exactly what I had said to Diane when she called before bed. I muttered a curse. Our telephones were bugged.

"It wasn't my fault," Turk responded.

"Well, that don't make no difference. He tells you to whack her, you whack her—or *you* get it, understand?" He cleared his throat. "He's already got three under his belt. A couple more ain't going to make no difference. Gimme that bottle. I want another drink."

"When are we going to know something?"

"Why don't you settle down? He'll send somebody out here later. Then we'll know." I could hear the agitation in Buzz's voice.

"He could call on his cell."

"He could, but he won't. You know that. And I ain't about to call him."

A cold chill had settled over me. I felt around in the dark for the chain and picked it up, holding it so the heavy padlock was on the end, a formidable weapon.

Feeling the weight of the padlock in my hand, I peered through the crack in the door.

A blinding flash of lightning followed instantly by an explosion of thunder shook the house. The light in the hall flickered once or twice, then went out, plunging the floor into darkness.

Excited curses rolled up the stairs. From what I heard, it seemed the electricity was out throughout the house.

Buzz shouted, "Stop griping. Use your cigarette lighter and see if you can find some candles or a lantern. Old place like this is bound to have something."

Arms extended, I eased across the hall and felt my way along the wall to the first door. I opened it slowly in an effort to keep it from squeaking, although in all probability, any sound would have been lost in the noise of the storm raging outside.

Lightning cast a brilliant white rectangle across the floor and bed, illuminating Diane's shoulders and face. I slipped forward and, in the next explosion of light, placed my hand over her lips. "Diane! Diane! It's me, Tony!"

She jumped and slammed my hand away instinctively before realizing I wasn't one of her abductors. "Tony?"

I sat on the bed. "Yeah. You all right?"

"My head hurts, and I feel sick to my stomach."

"That was the chloroform they gave us." I took her arm. "Can you get up?"

"Yes. But where are we?"

"I've got no idea. Some old house way out in the middle of nowhere. Electricity's off. All I know is we've got to get out of here. Buzz and Turk are downstairs." I didn't go into detail.

She sat up and groaned. "My head is killing me."

"Forget about it. Come on, but stay on tiptoe. We're on the second floor. They can hear any noise up here." I took her hand. "Follow me."

Using the brief flashes of lightning to show us our way, we eased from the room and down the pitch-black hall to the top of the stairs. I turned to her. "Wait. Let's try to find out where they are."

"All right," she whispered.

Looking down the hall, I caught a glimpse of the stairway. It swept down to the foyer in a graceful curve.

Through the darkness I caught the tiny glow from a cigarette lighter as Turk came through a doorway and crossed the foyer at the bottom of the stairs. "I ain't found no candles yet," he called out as he entered an adjoining room. "You find anything?"

From deep in the rear of the house, Buzz replied, "No. Keep looking."

I flexed my fingers about the chain, swinging the padlock back and forth just in case. "Easy," I whispered. "We're going downstairs and outside if we can."

"Outside?"

"The van. I'll hot-wire it, and we'll get out of here."

Diane halted abruptly. "What if he comes back?"

All I could do was tighten my grip on the chain.

Chapter Twenty-two

Holding our breath, we eased down the stairs. When we were halfway across the foyer, a dim yellow light appeared in the darkness of the room off to our right, heading straight toward us.

I pushed Diane against the wall beside the open door and then seized the chain with both hands. Just as the faint flame appeared in the doorway, I swung the chain and padlock.

The heavy weight caught Buzz on the forehead, sending him staggering back into the living room. I jerked Diane after me. "Quick. Let's go."

Just as I wrenched open the door, Turk shouted, "Stop, or I'll shoot!"

I yanked Diane onto the porch and shoved her to one side of the door. I leaped to the other.

Turk charged out the open door after us. I lunged at his back, shoving him as hard as I could down the ten-foot flight of steps to the ground below. Lightning lit the sky as he sailed through the air and hit the ground hard. He lay motionless.

I waved at Diane. "Quick. The van."

We sloshed through the water and mud to the van parked on the graveled circular drive and jumped in. The driving rain pounded the metal roof, and lightning crashed on every side. Diane shouted for me to hurry.

To my surprise, the keys were in the ignition. The engine roared to life, and as I jerked the transmission into drive, a hole exploded in one side of the windshield. I didn't hesitate. I jammed the accelerator to the floor, and the van fishtailed around the curve and along the drive toward the road, the headlights struggling to penetrate the driving rain.

Just before we reached the road, another set of headlights turned down the drive, heading in our direction. They blinked several times, signaling us to stop.

"Don't stop!" Diane shouted, sitting on the edge of the seat and clutching the dash so hard, I'm certain her nails left deep gouges.

"Don't worry about that!" I exclaimed through clenched teeth as I fought the gumbo mud trying to rip the steering wheel from my fingers.

We shot past the car. I caught a glimpse of the driver in the beams of my headlights. I wasn't certain, but he reminded me of one of the pool players back at the Golden Crystal Casino, the one they called Mule. If that were true, that meant the "he" that Turk and Buzz had spoken of could be Anthony O'Donnell. Otherwise, what was Mule doing here?

In the side mirror, I saw the vehicle's brake lights flicker and then go off as it raced toward the house.

Diane craned her neck around like a stork's. "He stopped at the house," she shouted.

By now, we had reached the road. I turned right, hoping I wasn't taking us into a dead end.

"He's coming, he's coming!" she shouted. "Faster, Tony, faster. He's coming."

I shot a quick look in the side-view mirror, just as the car burst from the drive and fishtailed from shoulder to shoulder on the slick macadam road. "See if there's anything in the glove compartment we can use."

She opened the door, and in the light emanating from inside the compartment, I spotted the butt of a pistol. "There's a gun!" she exclaimed, pulling out a snub-nosed revolver. It looked like a .38. I knew from our time together, she knew nothing about guns. That was then. This was now. "You ever learn to shoot a pistol?"

"No."

I took it from her and tucked it under my belt. "Great," I mumbled.

We were racing down the road, too fast for my comfort, but there was no choice. The darkness and the rain enveloped us, muting the glare of the pursuing headlights.

Our own headlights carved out a fuzzy cone less than a hundred feet before us. Instinctively, I slowed. Rain and wind whistled through the hole in the windshield.

My only consolation was that those behind us were facing the same problems. "Find something to stuff in the hole in the window."

Fumbling behind the seat, she found several rags and stuffed them into the hole. Her breathing was shallow. "Tony, they shot at us."

I kept my eyes on the road. "Yeah."

Her voice was strangled. "You think—I mean, were—"

Flexing my fingers about the wheel, I muttered, "I don't know. Not now."

She moaned.

To my relief, the narrow macadam road angled back to the northwest, toward I-10. A sign appeared on the right: PIRATES LANDING, 2 MILES. I looked at my watch: almost four. Another sign appeared, warning drivers of a series of S-curves ahead.

The reddish glow from the dash lights emphasized the fear scribed over Diane's face.

I took the curves as fast as I dared. We whipped around a sharp curve and shot into the small village of Pirates Landing. Except for an all-night convenience store, the town was closed down. A single flashing caution light hung in the middle of a four-way intersection.

Half a block beyond the intersection, the road curved back to the south. A car lot faced the curve. Behind the lot, a shell road cut back east. I braked quickly, then turned off the macadam and pulled into the shadows behind the car lot's service garage. From where we sat, we could see the front of the convenience store through a row of storm-battered trees.

Diane shouted in alarm. "Why are you stopping?"

I turned off the lights but kept the engine running. "I'm guessing there's only one car. Whichever way it goes at the intersection, we'll head back the way we came."

The shadows hid her face, but I could imagine the disbelief on it when she exclaimed, "The way we came?"

"I figure that's the last thing those bozos would think of." Headlights slashed through the rain, and a tan car slid in at the convenience store. The front right fender had several deep scars along it as if it had scraped a fence post. I learned later it was a Lexus, but my recognition of automobiles was limited to Chevrolet Silverado pickups. All of the boxy shapes or extreme curves of contemporary cars looked the same to me.

A figure jumped out of the car and rushed inside.

"Turk," I muttered.

Diane was breathing hard. She was whispering under her breath. I couldn't make out what she was saying, but I sure hoped it was a prayer for us.

Turk raced from the store and jumped into the Lexus, which then sped northwest. I pulled out from where we were hiding and headed back in the direction we had come from.

Several miles beyond the antebellum mansion in which we had been held prisoner, I took the first hardtop back to the north, hoping to hit I-10 somewhere.

According to the radio, the storm would continue until at least midmorning. Flood advisories were out for all the low-lying areas of the state, which was pretty much everything south of the interstate. Grimly, I hoped we wouldn't run into a low-water crossing.

I glanced at my watch: almost four thirty. Another hour or so before the first gray glimmers of false dawn. Keeping my eyes on the winding road ahead of us, I said, "We've got to ditch this van somewhere." From the corner of my eye, I saw Diane look around at me. "They'll be looking for it, so we've got to drop it off someplace where they won't find it too fast. That'll give us time to get back to Priouxville. We can't go back for the Cadillac. They'll be watching it."

Her voice quavered with fear. "You keep saying 'they.' Who are *they?*"

"I don't know," I lied. "So much has happened in the last couple of days, I haven't had time to sit down and think about it. All I want to do is get us safely back to Priouxville."

We eventually hit the I-10 access road, which curved beneath an overpass and led us into Bon Espoir, population fourteen thousand. The name was French for "good hope." I crossed my fingers that fate was not playing another trick on us.

The amber glow of high-pressure sodium streetlights lit the four lanes bisecting the small city. The garish signs of several fast-food restaurants and convenience stores beckoned to their customers. Pickups and vans were most prominent about the early-morning gas stations and restaurants.

I pulled in back of a McDonald's and stopped. "Go in and get us a table." Diane frowned. "I'll park down the street," I explained.

She climbed out and then looked back in surprise. "My purse. I—"

I pulled out my wallet and handed her a couple of bills. "Forget it. No telling where it is. Just get us a table."

She closed the door, and I sped away. I found a spot behind a ShortStop convenience store on the next block and parked between two Dumpsters. I hurried back to McDonald's, making sure my shirt covered the revolver tucked under my belt.

Diane had found an empty booth near the rear of the restaurant. We each ordered coffee and a breakfast biscuit and kept our faces lowered while we ate and discussed our next move.

"We'll get a cab and find a motel."

"Motel?"

"Car rental places don't open until eight or so," I explained. "We can't afford to wander around out here for the next three hours."

"What about the bus station?"

"Huh?" I stared at her for a moment and hesitated. The idea appealed to me. It wasn't as high profile as car rental services or cabs. Besides, we could always sit next to an exit in the lounge in case the trio showed up. And on the bus, our faces would be among twenty or thirty others. "I hadn't thought about a bus." I slid out of the booth. "Wait here."

From the pay phone, I called the American Lines bus station. I wanted to shout when they informed me a bus would be pulling out for Houston, Texas, at six thirty. That meant we could make connections in Lafayette for Priouxville.

I told the clerk where I was and asked directions.

"You don't need directions. Look out the window. See the Moulin Rouge Motel across the street?"

I glanced out the window, spotting the green and red neon sign. "Yeah."

"That's it. The bus picks up passengers in the lobby here."

Ten minutes later, tickets in hand, we each poured a cup of coffee and made ourselves comfortable on a battered couch in front of a new flat-screen TV in the motel lobby, eagerly awaiting the arrival of our bus. From time to time, I laid my hand on the reassuring bulk of the .38.

I'd given the motel/bus clerk a story about hitching a ride from New Orleans with an acquaintance, saying this was as far as he was going. "I knew we couldn't hitch a ride on to Lake Charles, so the bus was our only choice," I explained.

A tall, skinny man with a shock of long black hair hanging down in his eyes shook his head. "Me, I know what you say. There be too many of them hitchhikers out there what want to hurt folks."

For the next few minutes, we made idle chitchat.

Diane hissed. I glanced at her, and she shifted her furtive gaze to the front window.

My blood ran cold. A tan Lexus had pulled up beside the red van in back of the ShortStop down the street.

Chapter Twenty-three

My heart thudded in my chest as I watched Buzz and Turk search the van and then disappear into the convenience store.

After a few minutes, the two emerged from the store and went next door to the donut shop. Their next stop was the McDonald's. Diane looked up at me in alarm when they pushed through the doors into the restaurant. I shook my head almost imperceptibly.

At that moment, a green and white bus pulled in under the portico in front of the motel.

"There she is, folks," called out the desk clerk. "American Lines, and believe it or not, she's early. Load up as soon as the driver gets the other folks' luggage."

The door hissed open, and a small man in a gray uniform with a service cap stepped down. Three passengers followed. He unlocked the storage area and found their luggage. He glanced around and grinned at the desk clerk. "Hey, Jimbo. Any riders for me?"

The clerk nodded to us. "Only two. They be going to Houston."

We handed the driver our tickets and climbed aboard. As we made our way down the aisle, I glanced out the window. The Lexus remained in front of McDonald's.

We found two empty seats in the rear of the bus.

I didn't lie to myself. Having found the van, those bozos would methodically run down every means of transportation out of the small town. The bus station was just a matter of time.

The smell of burning diesel grew stronger as we roared away from the Moulin Rouge Motel.

Diane sagged against my shoulder. "What a relief. Now we're safe."

"Yeah." I started to say more but held back. I had to figure out our next step. We were sitting ducks on the bus. Then I thought of Leroi, my cousin in Opelousas. He was only an hour from Baton Rouge. Finally, I relaxed, but only slightly.

We remained silent. Sometime later, I looked over at Diane. She was sleeping.

One unwavering fact I've discovered in the PI business is that events will never go as you plan. That's why I knew we had to get off the bus as quickly as possible.

I had an idea, one that would call for the aid of my cousin, Leroi. At our first stop, I would put my plan into action.

That job out of the way, I turned my thoughts to Eddie Dyson's message regarding Benoit's cell mates. He said C. K. Judice and Benoit had shared a cell. Lacoutrue's message had not included Judice as a cell mate. Why?

The only explanation that made sense was that the sheriff had assigned the task to his deputy, Paul Thibodeaux, who struck me as the kind who might go fishing without a hook.

If, as Eddie Dyson reported, C. K. Judice had spent time with L. Q. Benoit at Winn Correctional, then there was a good chance he'd revealed the secret of the hidden diamonds to the old man.

I grimaced at the dirty tricks fate sometimes played. The old man had probably returned to Priouxville figuring he would never again want for money in his life. Instead, someone had killed him and then left horse tracks in the mud to place the blame on the loup-garou. I leaned back against the seat and closed my eyes. I was exhausted, but I couldn't afford to sleep. Buzz and Turk weren't the brightest lights around, but their boss was no dummy.

We stopped a few miles up the road at a Super Go convenience store in Gonzales for a rest break. Inside, I got lucky and found a pay phone. I called Leroi.

He picked up on the first ring. "Catfish Lube."

"It's me, Leroi, Tony. Just listen. Don't talk. I need help. Bigtime. Fast."

Thinking I was joking, he quipped, "What's up, cuz? Rob a bank or something?"

"I'm serious, man. Some bad guys are after me and Diane. You remember her."

He grew serious. "Yeah. Your ex. What are you two doing together?"

"I'll explain it all later. We're on an American Lines bus. I don't know where the station is in Baton Rouge, but you remember the old Colonial Plaza on Highway 190, north of town? Carson's Supermarket was across the street. You know, where we used to deliver sweet potatoes when we were in high school?"

"That place still there?"

"It's a Piggly Wiggly now. At least it was last fall."

"I got you."

"Meet us there. About an hour or so. Don't leave without us."

"You got it, bro. How you going to get out there?"

"Don't worry about that. And, Leroi—"

"Yeah?"

"You still carry that .45 under the seat?"

"Sure do."

"Good. Don't lose it."

Back on the bus, I explained to Diane that we had to get off the bus as soon as we hit Baton Rouge. We couldn't take any chances. "I would not be at all surprised if those jokers aren't waiting at the bus station for us."

Her eyes grew wide in alarm.

"But Leroi's only seventy miles from Baton Rouge," I reassured her. "He'll be waiting for us when we get there."

She frowned. "Isn't he your black cousin?"

My eyes grew cold. "This isn't the time to turn your nose up at help. We need him now more than anything."

She eyed me a moment, then dropped her gaze. "I'm sorry, but what if he isn't there?"

I chuckled. "He will be. If he isn't, then we'll just be forced to do a lot of shopping at the Piggly Wiggly until he gets there."

For the next forty minutes, I kept looking for the tan Lexus with the scarred fender. Finally, we rolled into Baton Rouge.

The bus turned onto Highway 61 from I-10. At the first red light, Diane and I disembarked.

I glanced over my shoulder as we mingled with the pedestrian traffic.

"Now what?" she whispered.

"Now a cab." I saw a Checker down the street. "There's one now."

Just after we climbed into the cab, I thought I spotted the tan Lexus. I wasn't certain, but I pressed back in the seat to be safe.

The Colonial Plaza was north of downtown, near where the Opelousas Highway turned west and crossed the Mississippi.

Leroi was waiting for us. A broad grin split his face, his white teeth in sharp contrast to his black skin.

He didn't waste time asking questions. As soon as we got in and closed the door, he whipped his yellow pickup around and quickly shot up to the speed limit.

Chapter Twenty-four

In Opelousas, we picked up a vehicle from Pelican Rental, grabbed a hamburger and milkshake, and headed for Priouxville. An hour and a half later, we pushed through the door into Jack's room. He stared at us in surprise. "Jeez. You look terrible."

The tears Diane had been holding back finally came. She rushed to him and buried her face in his chest, sobbing uncontrollably.

He cradled his good arm about her and patted her gently on the back. He looked up at me, his face a mask of confusion. I shook my head and for the next fifteen minutes detailed the events of our trip to New Orleans and the harrowing hours we had faced.

"But who were they?" he asked furiously.

"I don't know for sure. The only thing I'm positive about is that someone thinks we know more about the diamonds than we do. I figure they're trying to run us off so they can search without interference."

"Run you off? But they shot at you."

"Yeah."

He muttered a curse through his teeth. "They tried to kill you."

What could I say? "Yeah. Maybe."

"Maybe?"

"They were mechanics. But if they'd planned to waste us, they would have done it, instead of chaining us up in that house." I don't know if I convinced him or not. I wasn't even sure I had convinced myself.

By now, Diane had stopped crying and was wiping away the tears in her eyes. "You've got no idea how scared I was," she said softly to Jack. "I kept thinking about you."

Jack grinned sappily. "I'm just glad you're okay."

She looked around at me in shock. "What about the car?"

"The car?" Jack looked from her to me.

I hooked my thumb in the direction of New Orleans. "It's still in Frenier," I said, reaching for the phone. "I'll give them a call."

A few moments later, the receptionist at Frenier Motors put me through to the service manager. I asked about Mrs. Edney's Cadillac and listened in disbelief as he replied that her husband had picked it up yesterday afternoon.

"What?" Jack exclaimed when I related the service manager's announcement.

With a wry chuckle, I replied, "That's what he said. You picked it up yesterday."

Jack sputtered. "Some no-good—"

"It's probably in the bottom of some bayou by now." I paused and then added, "Seems like the electronic ignition went out. The service manager asked me if anyone had been tinkering with it. When I asked why, he said it sure looked like someone had been messing around with it."

Jack frowned deeply, the layer of flesh across his forehead wrinkling. "So it was deliberate?"

"Appears so. They had to have done it while it was in the hotel garage. We never took it out once we got there."

Jack laid his head back on the pillow and slowly rolled it from side to side. "What now?" Before I could reply, he continued, "Maybe you ought to tell Sheriff Lacoutrue. He stopped in just after you left, looking for you. I told him you and Diane were headed to New Orleans."

I nodded absently, wondering why the sheriff hadn't stopped me in front of the hospital when he passed just before we pulled out for New Orleans. I shrugged it off. "I plan on telling him about it. And the Cadillac."

Jack glanced at Diane. "You and Tony go buy another car. Another Cadillac if you can find a dealership around here."

He winked at me. I rolled my eyes. What was the remark about the wealthy attributed to F. Scott Fitzgerald—"They are different from you and me"? He was sure right about that.

I followed Diane in my pickup back to Charenton, where we turned in the Ford rental car. From there, we drove back to Bayou Country Motors. "Might as well give them the business," I remarked when she asked why Priouxville and not Charenton.

Oscar Mouton was surprised to see us; he was even more surprised when Diane told him she wanted a baby blue Cadillac convertible; and she compounded his surprise by writing him a check for the vehicle. "But," he replied feebly, "I don't have it in stock. I'll have to bring it down from Lafayette—tomorrow, if they have one. The next day if I have to get one out of Baton Rouge."

She shrugged. "That's no matter. I'll take a courtesy car until then."

While we were waiting for the courtesy car, a tan Lexus pulled up in front of the service entrance and stopped. My eyes grew wide when I spotted the scars along the front right fender, just like those on the car that had pursued Diane and me early that morning. A man wearing a pair of gray khakis came out of the garage and leaned through the passenger's window. He and the driver exchanged a few words, and then he waved as the car sped away.

I caught my breath when I glimpsed the driver. It *was* Mule! I turned to Diane, but she was idly perusing a magazine. Before I could say anything, the courtesy car pulled up.

Peering out the window, I watched as the Lexus pulled onto the highway and headed in the direction of Priouxville.

Jack was dressed and sitting on the edge of the bed when we returned. "The doc turned me loose," he announced. "I can't wait to get out of here and sleep in my own bed tonight."

Diane glanced at me and then frowned at Jack. "What about those men? What if they come out to the house?"

Jack snorted. "Then they'll get a taste of my .38."

I wasn't crazy about the idea.

"Look," he said through clenched teeth, "wherever we stay around here, if they want to get to us, they can." He laughed softly. "They'll regret trying."

"Go back to Austin, Jack. Forget about this place."

He glared up at me. "No way. I bought the place. No one's going to run me out."

I turned to Diane, expecting her to agree with me. She surprised me again. "If Jack wants to stay, I want to stay."

They were both nuts. I didn't say as much, and I couldn't leave them. I drew a deep breath and released it slowly. "I'll report it to the sheriff and see about getting some security out there."

After he was released, Jack and Diane's first stop was the vet's to pick up Mr. Jay. I stopped at the sheriff's.

Sheriff Lacoutrue and his deputy listened intently.

When I finished, he glanced at Thibodeaux, then back at me. "You say the driver, he looked like the one called Mule?"

"Yeah. I couldn't say for certain. I saw him in a flash of light, but he looked like him. And then I saw him this afternoon in that same car out at Bayou Country Motors."

A faint smile played over the sheriff's face. "I don't know about this afternoon, but it couldn't have been Mule last night, Mr. Boudreaux. Him and Alton was here playing *bourré* with me. Thibodeaux here was off, so Mule and Alton, they come by to keep me company."

His announcement hit me between the eyes. I stared at him, stunned. My shoulders sagged. I deflated like a balloon. "But what about when I saw him driving the same Lexus this afternoon out at Bayou Country Motors? The front fender was scarred just like the one last night. There couldn't be two around like that."

The sheriff frowned. "That do be funny." He glanced at his deputy. "Tell you what, Thibodeaux. You run out to Bayou Country. You talk to old Mouton. See what's going on."

Without a word, the deputy left. Lacoutrue grinned at me. "Tell you what, you," he said. "I guess it be plenty spooky, especially out there on the bayou. To make you folks feel better, me and Thibodeaux will swing by your friends' place during the night. Guarantee you no one will bother you tonight," he added. "Soon as Thibodeaux comes back, I'll call you."

"Thanks, Sheriff. I appreciate that."

During the ride out to the house, I replayed the night before. I would have given good odds that the driver was Mule, but it couldn't have been. He was a hundred and fifty miles away at the time. I shivered, the hackles on the back of my neck bristling. But then, what was he doing in the Lexus this afternoon? I drew a deep breath and blew it out through my pursed lips. I had the feeling that the whole situation was getting out of hand.

Jack and Diane had not arrived when I pulled into the carport at the house.

There was no sign of any disturbance around the cottage. Oh, a few black feathers lay about the grounds near the bulwark. Apparently, some male grackle had paid too much attention to his courting dance and not enough to a sly alligator.

After opening the house, I wandered down to the dock and jumped into the powerboat. Plopping down on the bench, I stared into the dark swamp, letting my thoughts ramble.

I had just about convinced myself that Anthony O'Donnell was behind the beatings and, in all probability, the deaths of Benoit and his two drinking buddies, as well as the attempt on our lives. I had been searching for a lead that would point to the culpable party, and I thought the night before had given it to me.

I ticked off the reasons on my fingers. Mule was one of O'Donnell's boys; he drove one of the kidnapper's cars; and, thinking back, he could very well have been the long-haired man I spotted darting down that dark passage to an interior court on Toulouse Street.

But Lacoutrue's announcement had taken Mule out of the picture. All of my little theories were just that, theories, with no substance.

The only one left was T-Ball, the Neanderthal Cajun who had shown up over at Cocodrie Slough. From what I heard, he seldom visited there. Why that night? And he had asked specifically about me. He and O'Donnell had to know each other.

The latter owned the racetrack, and the former raised and raced horses. O'Donnell could have sent the big man over there.

A scowl wrinkled my forehead. But how did O'Donnell know where we were? Our trip was on impulse.

Frustrated, I closed my eyes and shook my head.

Both Benoit and Emerente swore by the loup-garou. I knew better. There was a logical explanation for the tracks, although if someone insisted I provide such an explanation for the mysterious lights I had witnessed out in the swamp, I couldn't.

Even if O'Donnell or Mouton were involved, I couldn't prove it. So, that was my next step.

I couldn't help thinking that O'Donnell was a more likely suspect. He owned the racetrack. T-Ball owned and raced his horses at the track.

If I wanted to whack someone and put the blame on a mythical spirit like this particular loup-garou, I'd figure out some way to rig a horseshoe onto the head of a sledgehammer and beat him to death.

Gruesome, I know, but when the medical officers examined the body, they would most certainly find imprints of horseshoes. The tracks around the body were a snap to make. Simply weld a rod to a horseshoe and make all the tracks you want.

The blaring of a horn jerked me from my musings. I looked around to see Diane climbing out of the courtesy car.

Inside the house, Jack plopped down in his favorite chair in front of the TV. "Boy, oh, boy," he purred. "It's great to be home."

I glanced out the window, feeling the reassuring bulk of my .38 under my belt.

Diane looked at me. "Did you see the sheriff?"

"Yeah. They're going to patrol the place tonight."

"Good." She put Mr. Jay down and patted Jack on the shoulder. "Just you relax now. I'll whip us up some dinner." She waved a slip of paper. "The hospital sent me your diet. How does chicken, sweet peas, and mashed potatoes sound?"

Jack grimaced up at me. "That strained stuff?"

"You can't chew, sweetheart. You know that."

Shaking his head slowly, Jack grunted. "I know. Yeah, strained chicken sounds great. Put a lot of butter in the potatoes, okay?"

Diane laughed. "Whatever you want," she called over her shoulder. "I'm just glad to have you home." Mr. Jay tagged after her, yapping all the way.

Jack groaned. "You've got no idea what I wouldn't give for some decent food." He made a face. "Can you imagine, strained chicken, strained peas, and strained mashed potatoes?"

I glanced in Diane's direction. "Where's your .38?"

With a smug grin, he opened the drawer of the lamp stand next to his chair, revealing a chrome revolver. "Right here. What did the sheriff say?"

"He's looking into it. Like I said, he'll have some security out here tonight."

Jack glanced in the direction of his wife. "Good."

A knock from outside interrupted us. I answered the door and stared in surprise. It was old Rouly. He gave me a gap-toothed grin. "I heard my neighbor's back home."

Chapter Twenty-five

I opened the storm door. "Come on in. He's right in here."

The old man removed his battered straw hat, dutifully wiped the mud from his boots, and then hobbled in and shook Jack's hand, assuring him that during his absence, the old man had looked after his place. "Never did find out who worked you over, huh?"

Jack hooked his thumb at me. "Ask him. I've been in the hospital."

Hearing the voices, Diane stuck her head through the doorway. Her eyes grew wide, then narrowed suspiciously when she spotted the old man in his soiled and threadbare clothes.

Old Rouly nodded to her. "Ma'am."

Jack gestured to a chair. "Have a seat."

The old Cajun shook his head. "Can't stay long. Just wanted to tell you, if you need something, let me know."

Diane's eyes softened, and a faint smile played over her lips.

Jack replied, "Thanks. You sure you don't want to sit a spell? We can put some coffee on to boil."

Rouly looked around the living room. "Nope. Me, I'm fine. Right nice place you folks got here. Old man Prioux what built the place first back down the hill wouldn't recognize it." He shook his head. "Yes, sir. Fine place." He looked back at Jack. "Don't forget. Give me a shout if you need something." He took a step back and glanced at Diane. "Ma'am."

I accompanied him out onto the porch. "I suppose you knew L. Q. Benoit pretty good, huh?"

He reached into his pocket and pulled out a plug of Red Man's

Totem tobacco and cut off a corner with the wicked-looking six-inch blade of his pocketknife. He offered me a chunk, but I declined.

He started down the stairs, working on the tobacco a few moments before replying. "Yep. Him and me, we grew up here together."

"What kind of work did he do?"

Rouly stopped and looked around at me, raising a suspicious eyebrow. "Why you asking about that?"

"No reason." I shrugged. "Just been thinking about him. You know, wondering what he did to get sent up to prison."

With a faint smile, he started on down the stairs. I followed. "He was like me. Do whatever you can. Mostly he shrimped and crabbed."

"That wouldn't have put him in prison."

Rouly's eyes glittered in amusement. "You be right there, Boudreaux. Shrimping and crabbing won't put no one in prison, but stealing cars sure do."

"What did he do when he got back here on parole? I mean, usually there's a job waiting for parolees."

"He had a job with T-Ball at his horse farm."

T-Ball! That was interesting. "What did he do there?"

At the base of the stairs, Rouly cut across the yard to his battered 1949 pickup. "He never got a chance. He was killed two days after he come back."

I walked at his side. I didn't want to irritate the old man, even if it meant pretending I believed in the loup-garou. "Why do you figure the loup-garou went after—who was it?—Primeaux and—"

"Vitale. Charley Primeaux and Dudley Vitale," he said, supplying their names. His phlegmy old eyes grew suspicious. "I didn't figure you believed in the loup-garou."

I shook my head and stared out into the darkening swamp and lied like a dog. "There's things that we'll never understand. The more I think about it, the more I think you're right. I saw the lights out there in the swamp."

He smiled smugly and punched his sunken chest with a bony finger. "Me, I know I'm right." He made a sweeping gesture to the swamp. "There be spirits out there that we don't even know about."

"Yep. So, tell me. Why did the loup-garou go after those two?"

He pursed his lips. "The loup-garou take them what it finds."

"You mean it could have taken anybody?"

He reached for the door handle. "*Oui.*"

"How well did you know Primeaux and Vitale?"

"They come up from Morgan City—" He paused. "I don't know, maybe twenty years back. They got themselves a shack down on the bayou and bummed around town for what they could get. I figure that's how come old Benoit, he stole them cars. He was just shiftless before they come here, but he took up with them, and their ways rubbed off."

"So the three hung together?"

Old Rouly opened the door. "Thicker than gumbo mud. Two or three times, Primeaux, he visit Benoit up at the pen."

"Good friends, huh?"

He climbed behind the wheel. Before he slammed the door, he added, "Me, I always figured they was after the diamonds and that old Benoit had the ear of the Judice boys up in the pen. They was both killed about a year after Benoit went up."

I replied, "So, maybe Primeaux and Vitale weren't such good friends of Benoit after all."

"That be about right. I figure if the loup-garou, it hadn't got them two, they'd have took the diamonds and disappeared, with old Benoit still in jail."

I took a step back, noticing that the bed of his pickup was once again full of scrap metal. I gestured to it. "Looks like business is pretty good."

His wrinkled face broke out in a broad smile. "*Oui.* Ain't bad."

Before I went back inside, I walked the grounds, my hand resting on the butt of my .38 under my shirt. Nothing but crickets and mosquitoes.

In the house, Jack and Diane were watching TV and sipping their evening dinner through straws. She smiled up at me brightly. "Your dinner is on the snack bar along with a chocolate milk-shake."

The phone rang. "Grab it, will you?" Jack hissed.

It was Sheriff Lacoutrue, who informed me that it indeed was Mule driving the Lexus that afternoon at Bayou Country Motors. It was a casino vehicle. It got hit in the parking lot, one of the valets said. O'Donnell had ordered Mule to take it down and see about getting the fender repaired.

"Hit in the parking lot?"

"That's what they figure. Nobody saw it happen."

I thanked him and hung up. I *bet* nobody saw anything.

"Anything important?" Jack was looking at me.

I decided to wait until after Diane left the room to tell him the truth. "Nope. Just the sheriff reminding us they'd be watching the place tonight."

"Good." Jack nodded at the snack bar. "Get your supper and come watch the movie with us." His expression gave away his concern for their situation.

I patted the .38 under my belt and nodded. On the snack bar were two large glasses, one with the milkshake and the other with the concoction Jack was eating.

Diane spoke up quickly. "Hope you don't mind, but I thought we'd have the same thing as Jack tonight."

"Hey, it isn't all that bad," Jack exclaimed. "All mixed together, it tastes pretty good."

I looked back at the tall glass containing a revolting green glutinous liquid. *Nothing,* I told myself, *that looks like that can be any good.*

I looked back around. They were both watching.

Rolling my eyes, I shook my head and picked up my dinner. "Okay. Where do I sit?"

To my surprise, the green goo called dinner wasn't bad. In fact, it was almost tasty as long as you didn't look at it. I managed to get about half down before I turned to the milkshake. *Don't ever break your jaw, Tony,* I told myself, not looking forward to breakfast, which, according to Diane, would consist of tasty Cream of Wheat, yummy half-and-half, and sinful honey, all blended to drink through a straw. I wanted to gag. I'd take coffee and later on pick up a honey roll somewhere.

Thirty minutes later, headlights cut a wide swath through the darkness, and the sheriff whooped his siren to let us know he was there.

That night, I lay awake in the front bedroom staring out the window at the vast array of glittering stars splashed over the dark. The hum of the air conditioner was a soft, steady purr, its monotony seducing one to sleep. I sat up and peered out the window. Nothing seemed to be stirring.

I went back over my little theory regarding O'Donnell. With Benoit in the same prison with the Judice brothers, and since they were well acquainted, the casino owner figured Benoit knew the location of the diamonds; and he also figured that since Primeaux had visited Benoit in prison, the old man had probably made him aware of the location. Back in town, Primeaux would probably have revealed the location to Vitale.

When O'Donnell failed to elicit the information from the two, he arranged for T-Ball to offer L. Q. Benoit a job on his horse farm to aid in the old man's gaining parole.

There was also the possibility, though unproven, that O'Donnell had somehow learned we had gone over to Cocodrie Slough and sent T-Ball after us—well, after me.

And then there was Oscar Mouton, Al Theriot's ex-partner and old friend. I didn't know what his relationship with T-Ball was.

Outside, a bull alligator bellowed.

I squinted into the night. A pair of headlights appeared down the road. The vehicle swung into the yard and turned around. It was a police cruiser.

I relaxed slightly, thinking back over my neat little idea regarding the casino owner, looking for holes. I didn't see any. And that worried me. There are always holes in a theory, and if there are none, my experience has been that the premise, the theory, was nothing more than a pie-in-the-sky dream.

Chances were, that was an apt description of Mouton's involvement, but still, I planned to delve deeper into his situation.

In all honesty, I had nothing hard and fast regarding either one. I just had to keep working at it. More than once, I'd floundered around on a case and, after fifty dead ends, stumbled onto the answer.

Taking a deep breath, I closed my eyes and tried to clear my mind and relax. The last thing I remembered was wondering just how I could prove any facet of my theory—in time to keep me from feeding the alligators.

I awoke the next morning not one iota closer to an answer than when I dropped off to sleep the night before. Then I caught a whiff of the mouthwatering aroma of frying sausage. I closed my eyes and groaned at the thought of perfectly good sausage being puréed into an unrecognizable liquid as thick as Elmer's Glue.

The front door was open. I glanced outside at the still bayou. *Another hot day,* I told myself.

To my surprise, Jack was at the stove frying up sausage and eggs. He smiled when he saw me. "Just because one of us has got to eat baby food, that's no reason for everyone to eat it. I figured you and my wife would like something solid this morning."

I could have kissed him. I glanced around the kitchen.

"She's still asleep," he said, turning back to the stove. "Coffee's ready. Grab some." He picked up his coffee and sipped some through the straw. He pointed his spatula at the round patties crackling in their grease. "I don't know if it'll work or not, but I'm going to do my darndest to purée some of this stuff. If that works, a rib eye steak is next on my list."

A few minutes later, he slid a plate of eggs, sausage, and biscuits in front of me. "Eat up." I glanced toward his bedroom. He laughed. "She always sleeps in."

How well I remembered.

Jack hefted his bulk up onto a bar stool with his coffee and a glass of half-and-half, sausage, and egg puréed into a grayish color. He eyed the concoction warily and then sipped it. A grimace contorted his face, and he shivered from head to toe. "Jeez, that's terrible."

"Put some honey in it," I replied, cutting off a chunk of sausage. "Maybe that'll give it some flavor."

He shot me a dirty look but promptly took my suggestion. "It isn't much better. But it'll have to do."

I shook my head. "Sorry."

"Don't be. Just enjoy your breakfast. Don't even think about me while you eat your eggs and sausage and sop your biscuit."

Around a mouthful of biscuit, I replied, "What are you trying to do, make me feel guilty?"

"Yeah," he chuckled, and then grew serious. "Now, about what you were telling me yesterday."

A knock at the door interrupted us. It was Clerville Naquin, carrying a covered platter of food.

Chapter Twenty-six

Jack invited him in for breakfast, but the slight Chitimacha Indian declined. He extended the platter. "We hear you back home, so my wife, Zozette, she fry up shrimps for you. They got a big, thick crust."

I swear I could hear Jack groan in misery. Crusty fried shrimp, his favorite, and he couldn't take a single bite. For a moment, just a moment, I considered suggesting Jack purée it, but I hated to add insult to injury. Instead, I repeated Jack's invitation. "You sure you won't join us?"

Clerville shook his head. "Me, I got work. You take care. You need something, just let me or my boys know."

Jack forced a weak grin. "Thanks."

I spoke up. "I want to thank your boys again for taking me over to Cocodrie Slough the other night. I hope Valsin wasn't too tired to go to work the next morning."

Clerville waved his hand. "*Mais, non.* The casino, it call after you leave. They not need Valsin that next day."

The casino! I tried to hide my excitement. As casually as I could, I replied, "Oh, that's where he was going to work, huh?"

"*Oui.* That one, he help park the cars. I tell them I give him the message, that he take you over to Cocodrie Slough."

I couldn't believe my luck. Here I was, sitting on the thin edge of frustration, when Clerville Naquin's unexpected announcement suggested that O'Donnell could have learned that I was across the swamp at the little village on Duck Lake and had sent T-Ball to scare me off.

While Jack carried the platter of fried shrimp back into the kitchen, I walked Clerville to his boat at the dock, giving me time to ferret out a little more information. "Valsin work at the casino often?"

"*Oui,* weekends, and then during the week when one of the regulars is off." He shook his head. "Don't pay as good as shrimping, but it be more regular, even if they be some bad ones over there. You know what I mean?" He looked up at me.

"Yeah. I know." I paused, then nonchalantly remarked, "I'd guess that there would be work over at Bayou Country Motors."

Clerville agreed. "Old Oscar, he got himself a good business."

"I heard somewhere that Oscar and O'Donnell were partners in the car business." That was a bald-faced lie, but I had long ago discovered that such a trick can sometimes elicit information without arousing suspicion.

Puzzled, Clerville frowned up at me. "Where you hear that?"

Playing the innocent, I shrugged. "I don't remember. Might have been in the waiting room at the hospital."

He chuckled. "No, them two, they not partners, but Oscar, his company takes care of the casino's cars and trucks. Every year, O'Donnell, he trade in his cars on new ones."

"I see."

From the swamp came the purr of an outboard engine. "That Valsin?"

He shook his head. "He out at Six Mile Lake."

"Well, I hope he catches a lot."

"That be good." The smile faded from his weather-browned face, and he ran his work-scarred fingers through his full head of thick black hair. He gazed wistfully into Ghost Swamp. "One day, he ain't going to be able to shrimp no more, not because he gets old, but because the swamp, she changes; she grows smaller, and the shrimp and crabs, they leave. The casino job, it be only one an old man can do."

"Have you ever thought about it?"

My question jerked him back from the reverie into which he

had momentarily slipped. "Me? No. Me, I be lucky. I die shrimping." His eyes clouded over. "I wish the same for them boys of mine, but I don't think that happen."

As he sped away from the dock, I couldn't help feeling sorry for the little man and his family—a family, like so many others, forced to look on helplessly as a way of life vanished.

After he disappeared around the first bend upriver, I turned back to the house. I was tempted to call Jimmy LeBlanc down in Terrechoisie Parish, but I didn't want to take the chance that he'd tell me to back off. Running down a missing person was one thing; snooping around a case that could involve multiple murders was something else.

No, I told myself, I had to do this on my own. If I could find one piece of hard evidence that supported my little theories, I would bring it to Sheriff Lacoutrue. He'd take it from there.

But what evidence? I had no idea.

When I found myself in such a situation in the past, I'd just barged ahead, hoping I'd stumble over something that I could use. I drew a deep breath. I knew I was fumbling in the dark, but to be honest, I had no idea where else to go.

I paused at the base of the stairs to the gallery around the house and admired the ornate balusters supporting the handrail on either side of the steps. That they were hand carved was obvious, for none of the fleurs-de-lis decorating the stair balusters matched those of the porch railing, all of which had been machined in exact detail.

Even though I wouldn't have done it, I could see why Al Theriot had insisted on salvaging the material and reusing it. Such artwork could never be matched or duplicated.

Jack was in his easy chair watching the national news on TV. He looked up. "So, what's on your agenda today?"

I hadn't really made any plans. On impulse, I replied, "I was thinking about going to the horse races. You and Diane want to go?" I figured once we got there, I'd excuse myself and nose around.

He sat forward gingerly. "Why not? Beats sitting around here."

Diane hesitated, then gave in to Jack's pleading. "Sure! I've always wanted to go to one."

Being a Saturday, the track hosted both an afternoon and an evening card. We arrived early, joining in with some of the more adventuresome sightseers strolling the paddocks and stables and taking in the pre-race preparations, a sight as entertaining as the races themselves.

The sky was clear, and the sun baked down. Realizing we would be at the mercy of the searing rays for two or three hours, we wore long-sleeved shirts, broad-brimmed straw hats, and sunglasses.

We toured the paddock and stable area for about half an hour, stopping occasionally to watch handlers work with their horses, all magnificent specimens. When Jack announced that he was growing tired, we headed back to the grandstands, walking the edge of a broad concourse where the horses made their way from the stables to the paddock.

I stiffened. Across the concourse, leading a feisty roan carrying a jockey in red and white silks, strode T-Ball. On the back of his red shirt was the logo T-BALL STABLES. I watched as he looked around, his gaze sweeping over me. I stiffened, then realized he wouldn't be able to recognize me in the getup I was wearing.

An idea hit, but first I had to figure out how to get rid of Diane and Jack.

When we reached the grandstands, I noticed an expanse of glass at least fifty feet high and as long as a football field above the grandstands—the racetrack's clubhouse. "That's where we need to be," I said, motioning toward the air-conditioned interior.

Neither argued.

The clubroom was laid out like stair steps, each level three feet above the previous. The top level held betting windows and two bars. The other levels were filled with tables, allowing customers to relax in air-conditioned comfort and observe the races through expansive windows.

After paying the waiter for our pitcher of draft beer, three mugs, and one straw, I excused myself and headed back down to T-Ball's concourse of stables. I wasn't sure what I was looking for, and I wasn't even sure I would recognize it if I stumbled over it.

Down in the paddock, I stopped a young man leading a prancing sorrel. "I heard T-Ball Stables had some nice-looking quarter horses. You happen to know where they're stabled?"

"You want fine quarter horses, mister, you come over to Chretian Stables north of Cankton. Up there, we got the finest horseflesh in the state," he said, and then pointed me in the right direction.

I made my way through the maze of stables until I spotted the one T-Ball was using that day. Casually, I strolled past, searching for the big man. Although the stables were busy, he was nowhere around. Probably, I guessed, taking in the first race.

A couple of young men were walking two of the horses, a strawberry roan and a gray. A third boy was hooking up a black to a walker.

I looked on as they took their ponies through their exercises. A fourth young man pushed through the stable door and nodded at me. "Hey."

I held up my hand in greeting. "How you doing?"

"Great."

"These horses are all part of T-Ball Stables, huh?"

"Yep." He looked at the three horses proudly.

"Best-looking I've seen today."

He threw out his chest. "They should be."

"I'm new in town," I said. "Your farm around here?"

He hooked his thumb over his shoulder. "A couple miles back up the main road. Can't miss it. A big sign out front, T-Ball Stables."

One of the walkers shouted to him. He waved back, then looked up at me. "Well, see you around."

"Yeah. See you around."

After watching for a few more minutes, I headed back to the clubhouse, a risky plan forming in my head.

Chapter Twenty-seven

At times in my line of work, I'm forced to don various disguises, a practice the profession calls *pretext,* a politically correct term for "lying." In my repertoire of masquerades are city workers, insurance salesmen, truck drivers, reporters, teachers, and half a dozen other guises that enable me to ferret out information otherwise unavailable.

I hate to say it's a sneaky business, but truthfully, sometimes it is. It is usually worth the subterfuge. And to accompany each of these personas, I have all the appropriate credentials—driver's licenses and other identification germane to the position.

The only contact I had had with the bearded giant, T-Ball, was in a dimly lit bar filled with smoke. I had been across the room from him, facing away.

I figured that if I donned a gaudy Hawaiian shirt, a floppy straw hat like planters wore, sunglasses, camera, and the ID of a freelance writer, he'd never recognize me.

That night, I contacted T-Ball Stables under the pretext of a freelancer wanting to do a story on small racing stables for *Louisiana Quarter Horse,* a national magazine featuring top-notch quarter horses throughout the state.

Naturally, Jules Thibeaux, aka T-Ball, jumped at the opportunity.

I pulled up onto the shoulder of the highway outside of T-Ball Stables the next morning and took a few photos of the layout from the bed of my pickup. The complex of stables formed a large L, which faced an exercise area beyond which lay the track.

161

Climbing back into my pickup, I paused at the entrance and stared up at the arched sign spanning the drive. T-BALL STABLES was painted in bold, bright red letters on a white background. On either side of the logo was the logo of the stables, a horseshoe.

I drove through the whitewashed gates and down a short asphalt drive, parking in front of a small office building. I drew a deep breath, hoping he wouldn't recognize me.

As I climbed out of the pickup, T-Ball strode from the office. "Mr. Carson?"

Decked out in my tourist regalia, complete with sunglasses and planter's hat, I extended my hand. Would he recognize me from Cocodrie Slough? "I sure appreciate your agreeing to see me, Mr. Thibeaux. Especially on a Sunday."

He took my hand in a bone-crushing grip and shook it until I thought my arm was going to pop off at the shoulder. "It be my pleasure, Mr. Carson, my pleasure. And you can just call me T-Ball. All my friends do." He gestured to the activity around the stables. "This be a seven-day-a-week business. No Sundays off."

He didn't recognize me! A thousand-pound weight slipped off my shoulders. "I'm Joe."

The big man bubbled with excitement. "So, where do we start? You want to take some pictures first?"

I laughed and fished my digital camera and miniature recorder from my pocket. "I'll be taking pictures as we talk. I've got enough room on this for five hundred shots." I patted my pocket.

"So, where do we start?" he asked again.

"Let me get a few shots of you in front of the stables, and then you can give me the tour," I said. "Afterward, we'll go into the office and finish up."

As a youngster on Grand-père Moise's farm, I'd ridden my share of horses and cleaned my share of stables. I was no expert on Thoroughbreds or quarter horses, but I knew enough to realize he had some fine animals.

During our tour, I discovered that T-Ball was a hard taskmaster, constantly barking orders and demands at the handful of trainers and walkers working with his horses. I also learned he was a hard drinker, for it seemed that every time we turned a corner, he pulled out a bottle of Southern Comfort stuck back in a niche in the wall.

Remembering his manners after his first drink straight from the bottle, he offered it to me, but I declined. "Thanks, but a little too early for me."

So two hours, a hundred and fifty-three pictures, and at least ten shots of Southern Comfort later, we headed for his office. While I was duly impressed by his operation, I was doubly disappointed in the fact that while we visited and shot pictures of every stall with their fancy Dutch doors, Thermos water buckets, and swing-out aluminum feeders, as well as every tack room, I saw absolutely nothing to link T-Ball to the deaths of the three town drunks.

The only thing he looked to be guilty of was excessive branding. There was a horseshoe etched into the wood everywhere I looked.

I was disappointed and frustrated. I still had no explanation for why he'd come after me at Cocodrie Slough or who had sent him. But I had to play out my little charade.

The cool air in his office was a welcome respite from the heat in the stables, where, despite massive cooling fans, the humidity seemed to intensify the sweet pungency of the widely renowned aroma of Horse Stable No. 5.

He opened a small refrigerator. "How about a cold Coke?"

"Sounds good," I replied, plopping down in a chair beneath one of the ceiling vents spewing out cold air. He handed me one, pulled one out for himself, and chugged down several gulps, after which, naturally, he topped off the can with a healthy slug of Southern Comfort.

I whistled to myself, wondering just what condition the big man's liver was in.

He took another long drink and eased into the leather chair behind his desk. "So, now what?"

Continuing my lie, I replied, "I'll put it all together. I'll show it to you before sending it off. Any changes or additions you want to make, you can let me know."

"When will it come out?"

I gave myself a little breathing room just in case he decided to verify my story. "I haven't contacted the magazine about the article yet, but, given your reputation, I don't see any problem. There's usually a six-month period before it comes out. This is April. Probably October or November when it hits the streets."

The jangling of the telephone interrupted us. T-Ball held up his finger to excuse himself. He answered the phone. His eyes danced. "Sounds good. Bring it over." He hung up. "That be a friend of mine. Me, I be a gun nut. Pete, he run across an old revolver he wants me to look at. You know about guns?"

"Some. I've messed around with black powder."

"Lord, Lord," he exclaimed. "That be something." He rose and motioned for me to follow. "I got a black-powder revolver in my truck. I use it on rabbits and varmints along the road. Come see."

I wasn't particularly interested in the handgun, but I had to play out my sham. "Okay."

T-Ball strode across the hardpan to his Dodge Ram pickup, bright red and white like his racing stripes. He opened the door, slid the seat forward, and pulled out a gun belt wrapped around a black holster from which he extracted a revolver. "Army Colt." He handed it to me, butt first. "It isn't loaded. That one, it be my favorite black-powder handgun."

I turned the revolver over in my hands. It was not a genuine Colt, but one of those Italian replicas. Still, it appeared to be well made. I cocked the trigger and spun the cylinder. It purred like a kitten. Gently, I lowered the hammer and handed it back to him. "Nice piece of work," I replied.

He swung it around, pointing to an imaginary target in the distance. "I like to hunt rabbits with it."

I whistled. "You must be pretty good."

An odd look filled his eyes. "I usually hit what I aim at."

Chapter Twenty-eight

After driving out the main entrance of T-Ball Stables, I slapped the steering wheel in frustration. I'd gone out to the stables hoping to find something to link T-Ball with Benoit and the deaths of his two drinking buddies.

I'd found nothing.

"Maybe I was completely wrong," I said aloud, as I pulled back onto the highway into Priouxville. I glanced at my gas gauge. A quarter of a tank left. I decided I might as well fill up, so I pulled into Doquet's Stop N Shop in Priouxville. I spotted old Rouly's rusty truck at the gas pumps. He was inside.

While my tank was filling, I noticed that the bed of the old man's pickup was full of scrap metal. Had I not just come from the stables, I would never have recognized the branding iron sticking up from the pile. It was a horseshoe.

"Howdy."

I looked around as old Rouly approached. "How you doing today?" I asked.

"Can't complain."

"Looks like you got a full load."

"Yep. Going to haul it over to Lafayette tomorrow."

I nodded to the horseshoe. "You even got T-Ball as a customer, huh?"

He frowned, at first not understanding what I meant until I pointed to the branding iron. "*Oui*. Me, I picked up that stuff last night."

My pump clicked off. I started to turn to it when I took a

second look at the branding iron. A tiny bell rang in the back of my thick skull. There was something familiar about the iron.

Replacing the nozzle in the pump, I asked, "All that came from the stables, huh?"

He started around the back of his old Chevrolet. "*Oui.*"

"That looks like one of the branding irons T-Ball uses on his stock," I said, pointing to it.

"The handle got run over and bent up," Rouly replied.

I reached over and pulled it from the top of the heap. Sure enough, the handle was bent almost in half. I brushed the dirt from the horseshoe. There was something familiar about it, but what? "It shouldn't be hard to straighten. I wouldn't mind something like this on my wall back in Austin. You take five bucks for it?"

On the way back out to Jack's, I glanced at the bent branding iron beside me on the seat. What was it that seemed so familiar? I could have sworn I'd seen it before, but I knew I hadn't. In fact, the only horseshoes I had seen recently were those burned into the wood at the stables and the glossy pictures Emerente Landry had shown me down at the *Priouxville Bayou News.*

Then it hit me!

I slammed on the brakes and pulled to the side of the road. I picked up the branding iron. I studied the shoe, staring in disbelief at the leg that was bent out a few degrees.

Trying to still the pounding in my chest, I glanced at my watch: almost two. The newspaper would be open.

I turned around on the narrow road and raced back into town. It couldn't be, but then, what else would explain it?

At the *Priouxville Bayou,* I asked Emerente for copies of the two glossies, offering to pay for them.

She waved me off as she scanned the photos to her computer and printed them up on her photo printer. "Just you tell me for what you want them. That be the only pay I care about."

I figured she'd spread the word all over town. I didn't want to lie to her, but if I were wrong, I'd hate for the whole town to see the egg on my face. "I'm not sure," I replied. "I had an idea. If it pans out, you'll be the first to know."

She lifted a skeptical eyebrow. *"Oui."*

Back in my pickup, I compared the pictures to the branding iron. The horseshoe was identical to the tracks in the glossies. I brushed at the grime and dirt on the shoe once again. Three of the nail holes were filled with black dirt that clung to the metal. I looked closer, and my heart leaped into my throat. With a thumbnail, I scraped dirt from one of the holes, catching the black substance in the palm of my hand.

I leaned over and, working up a dribble of saliva, spit it into my hand. I worked the black dirt around.

I felt the blood drain from my face as the thick saliva took on a reddish tint. I leaned back in the seat and realized the importance of what I had just discovered. Maybe T-Ball was not involved in Benoit's death, but the stables were neck deep in it, for not only was there blood on the branding iron, but this branding iron appeared to be the very one that had made the imprints in the dusty road.

I tried to still the pounding in my ears, reminding myself that the blood could have many sources. But I didn't think so.

Of course, I couldn't positively link O'Donnell with the murder, but T-Ball Thibeaux would start squealing like a pig to dodge a charge of murder.

Now what?

Go to Sheriff Lacoutrue?

I wasn't sure, so I decided to contact Jimmy LeBlanc down in Terrechoisie Parish. I felt more comfortable with him than the sheriff, although the latter had always been cooperative and helpful.

But, before I contacted Jimmy, I reminded myself, I wanted to make certain I had all my facts in order so he wouldn't think I was playing Chicken Little.

First, those who had worked Jack over had demanded the location of the diamonds. Prior to that incident, three men, all close acquaintances, were killed, ostensibly for the diamonds.

One of the men, Benoit, was the cell mate of C. K. Judice, one of the three who'd pulled off the heist. Benoit was beaten to death, and someone left horse tracks at the scene, tracks made by the branding iron at my side.

One of the provisions of Benoit's parole was a job at T-Ball Stables. That and the branding iron linked T-Ball with the killing.

Clerville Naquin had told Anthony O'Donnell that Valsin had taken me across the swamp to Cocodrie Slough. Other than Clerville, O'Donnell was the only one who knew I was at the swamp village. T-Ball came looking for me specifically. According to Dolzin, the Cajun Neanderthal said he was looking for someone named Boudreaux. The only way he could have known I was there was if the casino owner had told him.

When I didn't scare, the casino owner sent Buzz and Turk to try again. I remembered their chilling conversation. "Well, that don't make no difference," Buzz had said. "He tells you to whack her, you whack her—or *you* get it, understand? He's already got three under his belt."

Three! Vitale, Primeaux, and Benoit?

O'Donnell had enough money. He wouldn't kill just for the diamonds, but he would to cover a murder or three murders.

I reached for my cell phone and then remembered it was down in some bayou along Plantation Road, along with Jack's Cadillac and Diane's purse.

Starting the engine, I headed out to Ghost Bayou. I'd call Jimmy from Jack's.

Jack and Diane were sitting on the porch in the shade, sipping cold Tom Collinses and enjoying the breeze from off the bayou. She offered me a drink, but I declined. "Later. First I need to make a phone call. Long distance. I'll have it charged to my number in Austin." I glanced at Jack, who laid his hand on his waist, an indication he was packing the .38.

The phone rang. Diane picked up the portable. Jack snorted. "It's been like that all day. Neighbors calling. My cell's on the snack bar. Use it."

"Long distance?"

"It's free. Besides, last time I talked to my banker, he said I can afford a few bucks."

I hesitated, hoping LeBlanc wouldn't take offense that I was butting into police business. After a couple of minutes wrestling with whether I should call him or not, I punched in his number.

He answered on the first ring. Before he could stop me, I outlined what I had learned and suggested I come down and go over it in more detail. I could be there in an hour.

To my surprise, he seemed amenable to my suggestion, although I could hear a hint of skepticism in his tone. Unfortunately, he had other obligations. The next morning would work for him, so we arranged to meet at his office at eight A.M. "But you know," he added, "you're going places where you shouldn't. If I didn't know you, I'd be tempted to hit you with an 'interference with public officials' charge."

"I know. Believe me, I didn't go out looking for this. It just seemed to fall on me."

He laughed. "Like things always fall on you?"

"Yeah."

After hanging up, I headed for the porch, where I found Diane still on the phone. When Jack spotted me, he motioned to a chair. "Sit. Might as well have a drink. Phone's been ringing off the hook: different groups at the church, around town, the ones who visited me in the hospital," he explained. "You know how small-town people are."

"Yep," I replied, plopping down in a chair and thinking of old Benoit. "Salt of the earth."

He pointed to the road. "Cops have been dropping by every hour or so. Nice guys. Diane feels a lot better."

I passed the next couple of hours on the porch with Diane and Jack, nursing a Tom Collins and filling them in with what little I had learned about the diamonds. I said nothing about the murders, for in truth, there was nothing to say until I had definitive proof.

Diane leaned forward, her hair falling over her forehead. She brushed it back behind an ear. "You really think those diamonds are around here?"

"Your guess is as good as mine. From what I've learned, everyone and his uncle has looked for them, with no luck. If they're here, Theriot hid them awfully well."

Jack grunted. "I don't think they are. I figure he hid them somewhere else, and they'll probably never be found unless someone just comes across them."

"Dumb luck, huh? You really think so?"

"Why not? It works for me. Just wait. Some lucky idiot will stumble over them."

At the time, I had no idea just how prophetic those words would be.

Chapter Twenty-nine

The sun was dropping below the treetops, brushing the evening sky with wide swathes of purple and gold.

As far as I was concerned, the search for the diamonds had been pushed to the back burner with the discovery of the branding iron.

I was so anxious for the next morning, when I could lay out my evidence to Jimmy LeBlanc, that I almost jumped out of my skin when the phone rang.

Diane picked up the portable receiver by her chair. "Yes?" After listening for a moment, she handed it to me. "It's Sheriff Lacoutrue."

Puzzled, I took the receiver. "Hi, Sheriff. What's going on?"

He explained he had just spoken with Jimmy LeBlanc, and the Terrechoisie Parish lawman had been ordered to take part in a massive drug sweep down in one of the parishes along the coast. "He asked me to take a look at what you got, Boudreaux. Why don't you come on up here, and let's see what old Jimmy, he was talking about."

I listened carefully for any hint that I had offended him by going straight to LeBlanc. Some lawmen in smaller parishes are extremely sensitive about such matters. More than once, I've witnessed solid evidence made inadmissible by lawmen whose ego was greater than their dedication to their job.

"Sure, Sheriff. No problem. I didn't want to bother you over nothing. I figured Jimmy could tell me if it was worth your time." It was a half-truth, and I knew Sheriff Lacoutrue realized it. Still, I had followed the obligatory liturgy of deference to local power.

I replaced the receiver and pushed to my feet. "Got to run in and see the sheriff," I announced.

Jack looked at me. "The sheriff?"

"Yeah. You remember hearing about that old man they found dead along the road sometime back?"

Diane's face grew pale. Jack frowned.

"Well, I might have run across something that was part of it."

"Like what?" he asked.

"Well, maybe the club the killer used on the poor old guy."

Diane grimaced and shook her head. "I don't want to hear about it."

"I won't be long."

As I headed up the road toward town, I glanced in the rear-view mirror and spotted Diane placing the receiver to her ear once again. One thing about small towns, they look after their own, even the newcomers to their little village.

By now, the sun had set, and thick shadows filled the woods and settled over the countryside as I sped along the narrow macadam road. I had spent many years driving the backwoods of Louisiana, but still the narrow tunnel of light burning a hole into the darkness ahead of me filled the interior of my Chevy Silverado with a feeling of claustrophobia. The darkness was so intense, the headlight beams were nothing but narrow cylinders of light without any side spill.

As usual, Main Street in Priouxville was empty except for two or three pickups down at Doquet's Stop N Shop convenience store. Old Rouly's battered '49 Chevy was one of them. The sheriff's cruiser was parked in front of his office. I pulled in beside it and climbed out.

With the glossies from the newspaper office in one hand and the branding iron in the other, I pushed through the door. The door leading back to the cellblock was closed.

Across the room, Sheriff Lacoutrue looked up from behind his desk. A broad smile spread across his angular face. "Ah, Boudreaux. How you be, *mon ami?*"

"Fine. You?"

He gestured to the chair across the desk from him. "*Comme ci, comme ça.* So, so." He paused, his gaze sliding down to the branding iron in my hand. "One of T-Ball's branding irons, huh?"

I drew in a deep breath. "Look, Sheriff. Hear me out. Then if you want to toss me out on the street, go right ahead. Fair enough?"

"Fair enough."

"All right." I plopped down into the chair, holding everything in my lap. "First, someone is trying hard to find the diamonds that Al Theriot hid before he went to prison. My friend, Jack Edney, was severely beaten in an effort to locate them. You know about that. Three or four attempts have been made to scare me off. Then someone thought I was getting too close to Benoit's murder. That's when they got serious."

I outlined T-Ball's visit to Cocodrie Slough, the falling chandelier in New Orleans, and once again the kidnapping with intent to murder as well as our subsequent escape.

"T-Ball came to Cocodrie Slough looking for me. The only way he could have known I was over there was from Anthony O'Donnell."

The sheriff pursed his lips. "Me, I don't understand."

"No one knew I was over there except Clerville Naquin. After his boys and I left, O'Donnell called looking for Valsin. Clerville told him where we were."

Sheriff Lacoutrue drew a deep breath and leaned back in his chair. He held his hands out to his sides. He was growing restless. "So?"

"So, that brings up the three town drunks who have been killed in the last few months. The first two, Vitale and Primeaux, were friends with L. Q. Benoit, who was in prison with the Judice boys before someone wasted them. Someone killed Benoit because they thought he knew the location of the diamonds."

I laid the bent branding iron on his desk. "Whoever did it got cute and tried to put the blame on that old superstition about the loup-garou. They did it by using this branding iron to make prints in the road."

"You think T-Ball, he kill Benoit?"

I shrugged. "I don't know. If I had to guess, I'd say yes, but there might have been others involved. He might not have known anything about it. The one certainty is that the branding iron that came from T-Ball Stables is the one that made the tracks in the road, and probably the weapon used to bludgeon Benoit to death."

Opening the folder with the glossies, I laid them beside the branding iron. "Take a look. See how the heel of the shoe angles out a few degrees? And look at the nail holes. The open holes in the shoes show up in the pictures, but the clogged ones don't. They're identical."

Lacoutrue looked over the glossies and the branding iron. I pointed to the clogged holes. "I'll bet when we have this analyzed, we'll find that the dirt in the holes is mixed with blood, and the blood will be L. Q. Benoit's."

"You might be right about that, Boudreaux," Lacoutrue said, an odd look in his eyes.

"I remember old Rouly telling me that Benoit had spent the evening at his shack. He had just come from seeing you and—" I froze, seeing the image of Sheriff Lacoutrue sitting at his desk and smiling up at me when he stated he had not seen L. Q. Benoit since the old man got back into town from prison. I stared in disbelief into the sheriff's eyes that were smiling up at me again, this time with a hint of malice.

"And what, Boudreaux?"

I stammered, trying to buy time to extricate myself from the deadly dilemma in which my big mouth had placed me.

Behind me, the door to the cellblock opened. T-Ball's guttural voice broke the silence. "I told you I thought Boudreaux was the reporter who interviewed me."

I glanced over my shoulder, staring into the leering face of T-Ball Thibeaux and the muzzle of a black-powder revolver.

The loose ends slipped together. I looked back around. That was why Lacoutrue had given me the wrong names of Benoit's cell mates. That's how Mule and his sleaze knew Diane and I had gone to New Orleans. Jack had told the sheriff when he paid Jack a visit the morning Diane and I left.

I muttered. "There was no *bourré* game."

Lacoutrue snorted. "Give the man a blue ribbon."

I tried to bluff my way out of my predicament. "Jimmy Le-Blanc knows I came to see you."

Pushing to his feet, Lacoutrue sneered. "Well, now, Boudreaux, maybe so, but all me and T-Ball know is you dropped in, gave us a couple of pictures, and headed back to Austin. Us, we never see you again."

"He'll never believe you."

The lanky sheriff rested his knuckles on the desk and leaned forward. The sneer on his face grew wider. "Oh, he'll believe me. You see," he added, "that one, he's my cousin. Distant, but still, he a cousin."

I gaped at him, and at the enormity of the odds of such a coincidence. The fact that Jimmy was black and Lacoutrue white meant nothing. I have a black cousin. Racial mixes within Louisiana families are a matter of common record, seldom given a second thought.

T-Ball jammed the muzzle of his revolver against my spine. I stiffened. "Put your hands behind you," the big man ordered.

Chapter Thirty

I had no choice. I did as he said.

Lacoutrue shook his head and reached for the handcuffs. "No. Hands in front. Put the chains on him just in case someone happens by when we're loading him into the cruiser." Quickly he snapped the chain around my waist and then looped the cuffs around it and shackled my wrists. He glanced at T-Ball, his eyes cold with anger. "We wouldn't have to do this if you hadn't played games with that blasted branding iron."

T-Ball glared at him. "Don't you be handing me that. You beat Benoit so he couldn't talk."

"The old man was stubborn," Lacoutrue snapped.

I had to ask. "What about Primeaux? Did you kill him because he wouldn't talk?"

The sheriff snorted. "That one, his heart gave out." He leered. "Vitale, he don't know nothing, but he was a witness. So there be no choice. Like now." He cut his eyes at T-Ball. "Bring my cruiser around to the side. We'll take him out that way. You bring his pickup."

While he was giving T-Ball instructions, I looked down at the handcuffs. Despite the fear squeezing my chest, I felt a hint of relief when I saw that the cuffs were Smith & Wesson. Most of their models were simple to pick—with the right tool.

"What do you plan on doing with him?" T-Ball asked.

Lacoutrue eyed me coldly and nodded in the direction of Ghost Bayou behind the jail. "The bayou there, it hides everything. *Oui?*"

T-Ball sneered. "*Oui.*"

By now, night had settled over the small town. Only a thin beam of light shone through the office door as the sheriff hustled me outside and shoved me into the backseat of the cruiser.

I fell to the floorboard. Behind me, he slammed the door. While the chain about my waist limited the range of my searching fingers, I felt over the floorboard for any wire I could use to pick the handcuffs.

With the right tool, I could be out of the cuffs in thirty seconds.

To my dismay, I found nothing I could use.

By now, we had pulled onto the highway and were headed out of town. I struggled to my knees and placed my hands on the seat. My fingers slipped into that crevice between the back of the seats, and my fingers touched a paper clip.

I could have shouted with joy. I squeezed the clip for all I was worth, knowing my life depended on the flimsy piece of tin.

Lacoutrue snarled, "Don't fight it, Boudreaux. You can't get out them doors. And ain't nobody out here to help you."

Scooting around in the seat, I glanced out the window. Through the giant cypress trees and drooping strands of Spanish moss, I spotted flickering lights off to my left in the bayou. The sharp beam of a spotlight swept past.

The headlights of my pickup, now driven by T-Ball, shone through the rear window.

I turned my attention to the paper clip. Quickly, I straightened one end and then felt for the keyhole on the cuffs. Inserting the tip of the thin wire, I bent it into a ninety-degree angle, turned it over, and reinserted it into the tiny hole. I pressed down on the clip, forcing the bent tip upward, releasing the ratchet. The jaw swung open. All I had to do was slip the cuffs from under the waist chain, and both hands were free.

Now what?

The back doors of the police cruiser could only be opened from the outside. I couldn't break and run when we stopped. Lacoutrue would put half a dozen two-hundred-grain slugs into my back, then toss me to the alligators. If I waited until we climbed into the boat, my chances were even slimmer. I stared through the half-inch steel mesh separating the front seat from the rear.

In the past, I'd always try to cheer myself that, when things were going south, they could always be worse. Now, for the first time in my life, I was truly in a situation where, for the life of me, I couldn't figure out just how things could be any worse.

Lacoutrue turned off the highway and wound down a narrow road toward the bayou. The headlights punched holes into the surrounding darkness, a darkness that seemed to have a life of its own, threatening, engulfing, ready to snuff out the last breath from a person's lungs.

As we approached a sharp bend in the road, Lacoutrue braked. He rolled down the window and waited. T-Ball pulled up beside us and lowered the passenger window. "What you want here?"

The sheriff pointed to a side road in front of us. "That leads to the bayou. It not be used much, and the water's deep at the bend. Drive the pickup in there. I'll wait here for you."

"*Oui.*" The big man disappeared.

Lacoutrue chuckled. "Okay, Boudreaux, you take a good look, you. This be the last time you see that truck of yours."

My blood ran cold as my pickup rolled past. I watched as the headlights jerked up and down. Then the taillights disappeared into the black water.

With the truck now submerged, T-Ball returned and climbed into the front seat of the cruiser. "That be done, Thertule. Now, we take care of that one back there, *oui?*"

We drove a little farther, and the headlights touched on a cabin on piers with a boathouse next to it.

The cruiser stopped in front of the cabin. T-Ball yanked open the back door. "Okay, Boudreaux. Out!"

I kept my right hand over my left wrist as he half dragged me from the cruiser. In my left hand, I still clutched the paper clip, just in case I needed it again.

There was no moon. I glanced around, wondering if now would be a good time to try to make my break. Maybe I could lose them in the thick pine forest.

Lacoutrue must have read my mind, for he jammed his Magnum into the small of my back. "You, don't even think it. You be dead before you take one step." He nudged me toward the boathouse. "Follow T-Ball."

T-Ball flipped on a flashlight. As we padded over the wooden walkways spanning the black water, I toyed with the notion of diving in, risking the possibility of alligators as opposed to the certainty of a bullet in the back.

The sheriff must've noticed me eyeing the water and grabbed the chain at my back and muttered, "You'd be dead before you hit it."

T-Ball opened the door to the boathouse.

"No lights," Lacoutrue said. "We don't want no one paying us a visit."

"*Oui.*"

By the tiny beam of the flashlight, we climbed into an ancient Wellcraft bay boat, a center-console rig about eighteen feet long. The sheriff shoved me down onto the bench in front of the console and growled to T-Ball, "Watch him. I'll get us out of here. Turn off the flashlight when we get out on the bayou."

He backed the Wellcraft from the boathouse and turned it around. The starlight cast the ominous swamp in eerie relief.

Remembering the lights I'd spotted earlier on the bayou, I hoped for the appearance of lights from approaching boats, but only darkness greeted me. The engine purred as it picked up RPMs, moving slowly into the shadows.

Mosquitoes swarmed us.

"We'll go back into the swamp," Lacoutrue announced. T-Ball peered over the bow as we sped across the bayou toward the towering cypress. The sheriff sneered. "I like you, Boudreaux. That's why me, I'll do you a favor and shoot you before we give you to the gators. Otherwise, we'd just toss you out to them."

If my mouth hadn't been so dry, I would have told him not to do me any favors. But the words stuck in my throat. Looking back, I saw that the few lights that had been visible from the shore were quickly fading. My heart pounding in my chest, I removed the loose cuff from my wrist, slipped it under the chain around my waist, and clasped my hands back together.

T-Ball turned to face me, his legs spread on the deck for balance against the bouncing of the hull from the light waves.

Chapter Thirty-one

I wasn't certain just what I was going to do other than play out the hand the next few minutes would deal me. Whatever it was I would do, it had to be soon.

The only light was the flicker of starlight through the canopy of cypress needles. I could see T-Ball leering at me.

"Just ahead," Lacoutrue called out over the purr of the powerful engine.

T-Ball grunted and looked over his shoulder.

It was now or never. I leaped forward, slamming my hands into his chest and knocking him over the gunwale. With flailing arms and a wild scream, he flipped head over heels.

Behind me, the sheriff shouted and the powerful boat whipped into a sharp turn, throwing me off balance. I slammed into the console, swinging the handcuff still fastened to my right wrist. I caught the sheriff in the forehead and sent him stumbling backward to the deck.

The screaming engine drove the boat in wild circles, bouncing off cypress trunks and scraping over cypress knees, wrenching shrieks of agony from the fiberglass hull. I clutched at the console with both hands. Behind me, Lacoutrue was thrown from side to side as the boat literally tore apart on the rugged cypress knees.

"You're a dead man, Boudreaux!" Lacoutrue screamed.

I turned around in time to see him pulling his revolver. I lunged at him, knocking the Magnum from his hand and sending both of us to the deck of the careening powerboat.

He dug his fingers into my throat. "I'll kill you. If it's the last thing—"

I slammed a fist into his face, smashing his nose. Blood spewed over both of us. I hit him again, sending him tumbling against the gunwale.

I jumped to my feet just as the bow of the Wellcraft smashed into a thick cypress, sending both of us flying through the night into the black water. Moments later, the boat exploded, lighting the swamp with leaping yellow flames. The blazing fire would bring every alligator within five miles.

Even before I hit the water, I was flailing my arms, swimming for the nearest cypress with all my strength. The towering tree couldn't have been more than ten feet away, but it seemed like ten miles.

Nothing had ever felt as good as the rough bark of the cypress against my palm. I admit I was scared when I was swimming, but nothing compared to the fear I felt those last few seconds in the water before I shimmied up the cypress, ignoring the more than even chance of running into snakes in the tree.

When I was about ten feet up, I looked down. My blood ran cold when I saw several wakes converging on the inferno.

From somewhere back in the darkness, I heard a scream and the churning of water. I searched the firelight for Sheriff Lacoutrue but saw no sign of him.

I clung to the cypress, my feet resting on protruding branches. The fire died away as the powerboat sank beneath the black waters of the swamp. I caught my breath when I spotted a wake moving away from the boat and toward me. There was just enough reflection from the fire to see the eight-foot alligator lift its scaly head and open its toothy jaws. I don't know if that sucker could see me or not, but there was no question in my mind that he knew that somewhere above him in that cypress was something good to eat.

Flexing my stiffening fingers about the branches to which I clung, I glanced over my head into the darkness of the tree above. If I could hang on until morning, then I had a chance. Maybe there was a fork above that would afford me a chance to rest.

A flickering of lights fluttered through the trees. Despite my disregard for local superstition, my first thought was of the *feu follet*. Then a spotlight cut through the thick stand of cypress trunks.

The strong beam wound its way through the trees, steadily growing closer. "Here! Over here!" I shouted, knowing chances were slim that anyone in the approaching boat could hear me.

Then I heard Valsin. "Boudreaux! Where you be at? Boudreaux!"

If I am ever fortunate enough to hear heavenly voices, they couldn't sound any sweeter than his.

"Valsin! Over here!"

The Ranger began to take shape in the peripheral glow of its spotlight. I made out Valsin behind the wheel and his two brothers, August and Dolzin, at his side.

Then the brilliant beam of light hit me.

"There he be!" one of the brothers shouted.

Skillfully, Valsin guided the Ranger forward, gently bumping the protruding cypress knees until the bow of the boat steadied against its trunk.

I lost no time in scampering down and stepping onto the bow. I grabbed each of them in a bear hug. "Where in the blazes did you come from? I figured I'd be out here for a couple of days at least."

August grabbed Dolzin by the shoulder. "Thank this one. He be shoeing one of T-Ball's horses when he hear T-Ball talk to the sheriff about dumping you into the swamp."

"That be right," Valsin added. "We call you at your friends', but them, they say you done gone to Sheriff's."

"By the time Dolzin and me get there, he was driving away," August put in. "Us, we see your white pickup behind Thertule's police car, so we follow. Valsin, he was following us in the boat. When we saw where he was taking you, we jump into the boat with Valsin."

"*Oui!*" August said, reaching under the console and pulling out a jar of moonshine. "We got lucky. That calls for a drink—what you say?"

Far be it from me to argue with the ones who saved my life. I reached for the jar. "I say, drink up."

A terrified scream interrupted us. Valsin grinned. "That be the sheriff," he drawled. "What you think, Boudreaux?"

"Probably." I squinted into the darkness behind us. "T-Ball fell out a good piece back."

Another scream ripped through the night. Sheriff Lacoutrue's voice seemed to rise two octaves. "Snake! I be snakebit! Cottonmouth!"

Backing skillfully through the cypress knees, Valsin followed the spotlight with his eyes as Dolzin used it to search the dark swamp. On a distant cypress, the beam found the sheriff, who was shaking his arm to throw off the cottonmouth.

The black snake went flying through the air, landing with a loud splash.

"Hurry!" Lacoutrue shouted. "Me, I got to get to the hospital."

Just before we reached the tree, Valsin throttled back. I looked at him. "What are you doing?"

He ignored me. "You want help, Sheriff? You tell truth about old Benoit and the others."

Panic filled Lacoutrue's eyes. "What—me? I don't know what you mean."

Valsin backed away. "Too bad."

I grabbed Valsin's arm. "You can't leave him. We've got to get him to the hospital."

The lanky young man leered at me. "Why? We all better off leaving him out here."

"No, no!" Lacoutrue paused, clutching his forearm. "*Oui!* Me, I tell you. It be T-Ball. He want Theriot's diamonds. He kill old Benoit."

Valsin backed farther away. "The truth, Sheriff. Me, I want the truth, the whole truth."

Chewing on his bottom lip, sheriff Thertule Lacoutrue wore a deer-in-the-headlights look on his face before dropping his chin to his chest. "*Oui.* Me and T-Ball, we plan it."

I spoke up. "What about your deputy, Thibodeaux?"

"No. He know nothing. He just dumb Cajun. He do whatever

I say." Lacoutrue went on to spill it all, incriminating himself as well as T-Ball and the latter's three thugs, Mule, Turk, and Buzz.

Thibodeaux met us at the boathouse, where I gave him the whole story. When I finished, Lacoutrue tried to crawfish, to back away from his confession, but all the deputy had to do was promise to threaten Mule, Turk, or Buzz with murder one, and Sheriff Lacoutrue saw the proverbial handwriting on the wall.

All we found of T-Ball was half his shirt.

To my surprise, when we dropped the sheriff off at the hospital, I discovered Jack and Diane in the emergency room. The doctors were fitting a cast onto his right leg from the knee down. Despite the pain, Jack was grinning from ear to ear. "What in the blazes is so funny?" I asked.

He winked at Diane. She cleared her throat. "You remember when we were talking about the diamonds earlier this evening, and what you said when Jack remarked, 'They'll probably never be found unless someone just stumbles on them'?"

"Yeah, I remember. I said it would be just dumb luck."

She continued. "When Valsin called and told us about the sheriff and T-Ball, Jack ran out of the house. He was going to the sheriff's office to help. He tripped and fell down the stairs, breaking his ankle." She paused for dramatic effect. "That's not all he broke. He shattered three of the balusters supporting the rail, the hand-carved ones. And guess what we found?"

I knew instantly, remembering Ramsey's recollection, *"I was visiting family over in Texas when the news broke that Eloi Saint Julian's had been hit. It was on every TV channel and radio station. Well, when I returned two or three days later, Al Theriot was waiting for me at the house."*

Of course, I said to myself. *That explains why Ramsey found Theriot at the house.* He wanted to be sure his diamonds were safely hidden in the balusters.

Before I could reply, Diane pulled a handful of diamonds from her pocket.

"Take a look," she said as the light sparkled off glittering diamonds. "Pretty, aren't they?"

I shook my head in mute wonder.

When we had been talking about the diamonds earlier, Jack had snorted, "I figure he hid them somewhere else, and they'll probably never be found unless some lucky idiot finds them."

I winked at my old friend and remarked, "Dumb luck, huh?"

And his response was, "Why not? It works for me."

"Does it ever," I replied. "Does it ever."